Like A Trip Through The Mirror

Like A Trip Through The Mirror:
Lesbian Love In Alternate Realities

edited by Kathleen Tudor

Circlet Press, Inc.
Cambridge, MA

Like a Trip Through the Mirror: Lesbian Love in Alternate Realities
edited by Kathleen Tudor

Copyright © 2014 Circlet Press, Inc.
First paperback edition, December 2014

ISBN 978-1-61390-132-8

Published by Circlet Press, Inc.
39 Hurlbut Street
Cambridge, MA 02138
www.circlet.com

Like A Trip Through The Mirror

Contents

Introduction

Alternate realities and other worlds; the green, green grass on the other side; the essence of the living 'what if'. What if you could step through a mirror and find yourself in another world—maybe a better one? What if your dream lover awaited you in a place you could only find by stepping out of the world you know and into the mystery of something else?

Alice isn't the only one to have gone through the looking glass, only to find something strange and wonderful on the other side. For as long as there have been humans to imagine the world in new and excitingly different ways, there have been dreams and stories of people who step over that imaginary line. What awaits them?

This anthology is all about exploring that invisible line—that mirror, that hidden portal—and the places and passions to which it might lead. Step into another world with our characters, and watch them live out their dreams and fantasies on the other side, whether for a short visit to Wonderland, or to change their lives forever.

When I put out a call for alternate reality erotica with a "through the mirror" title, I expected a flood of Wonderland retellings, but with the amazing authors that write for Circlet, I should have known better. Instead of retellings of familiar flights of fancy, I got unique, fascinating, erotic stories from a good handful of women. The relationships were beautiful and developed, the alternate realities creative and varied, and the use of mirrors both careful and delightful.

This anthology didn't start out as a lesbian one, but when so much of a good thing comes your way, what can you do other than go with the flow? And so I have, gratefully. I hope that you enjoy these sensual tales of women stepping into the unknown and embracing the love and lust they find... on the other side of the mirror.

Kathleen Tudor
December, 2013

The Universe Where Katie Lived
Annabeth Leong

Genevieve Harrison smiled at her lover around her last bite of risotto. "That was delicious, Katie," she said. "Thank you."

Katie had adorned the table with their old lace tablecloth and silver-filigreed candlesticks. She'd served the risotto and herbed chicken on their china plates. Her favorite sapphire pendant hung in the space between her light brown breasts. Genevieve took in the scene and grinned. All this effort meant Katie wanted to get laid.

"Come here," Genevieve murmured, allowing lust to deepen her voice. Katie's face glowed in the candlelight. She pushed back her chair and stood. Impatient, Genevieve reached for Katie as soon as she came in range of her arms, pulling her slim lover easily up and over the arm of her wheelchair and into her lap.

Genevieve slid her hands slowly and firmly up from Katie's waist, over her breasts, up her neck, and to the sides of her face. She pulled her down into a kiss, tasting a little of the white wine Katie had poured herself along with dinner. Genevieve's legs registered brief flashes of Katie's soft weight. To her lower body, Katie seemed like a dream, a whisper. She took on solidity somewhere around Genevieve's waist, where twitchy nerves frantically fired with the news of the other woman's proximity. And to Genevieve's questing fingers, powerful arms, and probing tongue, Katie was all real and all woman.

"I'm going to lick you for hours," Genevieve sighed into Katie's almond-scented black hair. "I'm going to make you come until you forget your name." She'd already started working on the zipper at the back of Katie's dress, wanting access to the full expanse of her lover's skin.

Katie smiled against Genevieve's cheek, but then drew back, a crease on her forehead wrinkling her otherwise unblemished face. "I thought," she said hesitantly, "that maybe I could do you, tonight."

Genevieve blinked, shock and dismay distracting her even from the very important task of undressing Katie. "Why?"

Katie bit her lip and smoothed Genevieve's hair in a familiar gesture of apology. Genevieve knew Katie well enough to read this—she was about to get a planned speech. Annoyed, Genevieve caught Katie's fingers and pulled them down into view. She raised an eyebrow, prompting her lover to get on with it.

Katie's face fell, obviously reading Genevieve's irritation with the same facility that her lover could read her. "I thought this would be nice." Oncoming tears trembled in her voice.

Genevieve sighed, wishing for the simple lust of a few moments before. She spoke as sweetly as she could. "It is nice. Very nice. You are very nice. And I want you. Let me take you to bed. We don't have to do anything complicated."

"Gen, that's not what I want. I want to make love to you. I want to make you come."

Genevieve restrained herself from pushing Katie off the chair. "You know I can't," she said. "The whole 'no sensation in the genitals' thing. It kind of puts a damper on orgasm." She hated the nasty tone that had crept into her voice, but couldn't help herself. This wasn't even about not having had an orgasm in more than three years. Katie had no idea what orgasm would do to her—to them. Katie could never understand that, and Genevieve had thought they were safe.

Katie's tears came, dripping at first, then flowing with increasing speed. "I can't live this way, Gen," she whispered.

Genevieve stared, her lungs going cold. "What do you mean? We have a nice life."

Katie shook her head desperately. "I'm so, so sorry about your accident. I'm so, so sorry that you got hurt this way when it should have been me. But I can't feel guilty about it anymore."

"No one wants you to feel guilty."

"What do you think I felt just now? What do you think I feel when you won't let me touch you? When I know I can't make you feel good?"

"Katie. Katie, I don't need that." Genevieve reached up for the soft black hair, but Katie flinched away, jumped out of the chair and far from her lover.

"I need that," Katie hissed. "I need it. You just don't get it, do you? What it's like to live with you?"

The ice in Genevieve's chest spread through her body. Her torso felt as numb as her legs. "What are you saying?" Genevieve whispered.

Katie bit her lip and folded her arms over her chest. The gesture pushed her breasts up and nearly out of the low-cut dress she'd worn, and regret surged through Genevieve again.

"What is it?" she pressed.

"I don't know." Katie's voice was barely more than breath. "I need to think." Genevieve closed her eyes. The leather strap of Katie's purse creaked as she slung it over her shoulder. A moment later, the front door slammed.

Genevieve lay on her back on their bed, naked. She lifted herself up on her elbows and looked down at her lower half. She knew it was part of her, that it shared her blood and breath, but she always felt surprised to see it there, alien, yet attached to her. By propping pillows behind her back, she managed an angle that allowed her to examine herself between the legs.

Gingerly, she prodded her outer labia apart. Pink flesh flowered forth, as it would on any woman, but it felt dry to Genevieve's touch. The doctors had told her about that, the one time Katie had forced her to speak frankly with them. Her injury inhibited her lubrication, not to mention what it did to sensation. They had reassured her that she could still conceive a child, still go through a pregnancy, still give birth. Katie had nodded eagerly through the litany, and Genevieve had felt selfish thinking she didn't care about any of that. All she cared about was Katie.

Her clit used to come to attention whenever she thought about it, and it still seemed unbearably weird to be staring at it, thinking about Katie, even, and see it tucked, dry and lifeless, beneath its hood. Genevieve pinched it a little, rubbed it. For a moment, she thought she felt the pressure of her own fingers, but then decided she might have imagined it.

Would she like to have an orgasm? Sure, she would. It had been a long time.

Did she want to have an orgasm? Definitely not. For three years, Genevieve's injury had protected her from the consequences of losing herself that way. The old romance novels used to describe an orgasm as falling off the edge of the universe, and as a teenager, Genevieve had discovered that, for her, this description was quite literally true.

She didn't want to fall off the edge of this universe. In this version of reality, her body had indeed suffered. But in this version of reality, Katie lived.

The way Genevieve remembered it, the man had come out of nowhere, taking Katie by the elbow with a smile that could have been friendly. A cool wind ruffled the flaps of his jacket, which seemed much too heavy for a pleasant summer night. Neon glow from late-night restaurants made it impossible to place the details of his face, to define the color of his skin or the shade of his eyes. He'd whispered something in Katie's ear, and Genevieve's lover had suddenly gone white and still.

"What's the matter?" Genevieve asked. The smile that had been on her face hadn't had time to wither yet.

"Genevieve, run!" Katie screamed, and Genevieve had done as she was told. It seemed impossible to disobey. Katie's voice contained the howls of the furies themselves. It echoed in Genevieve's ears and forced her limbs into motion. She had no idea when she heard the shot, but that chased her, too. She was blocks away before it occurred to her to stop.

Later, Genevieve learned how the man shot Katie in the back before taking her purse and running away.

The first time Genevieve had an orgasm, she woke up the next day to discover her mom had different hair. Impossibly different hair, long and dyed red rather than brown and cut short. It took a while to figure out the cause of this, of course, and a bunch more experimentation to determine how much would change as the result of each orgasm. Genevieve had always been glad she learned about this as a teenager, when the changes felt like adventures, and she didn't think all the time about what she might lose.

By the time she'd reached college, she'd had things fairly well calibrated. It seemed to take energy to travel to a different reality, and an orgasm could only provide so much. She never woke up with five hands, or surrounded by alien creatures.

Ordinary orgasms usually didn't change things too much. Afterward, she'd find different things in her closet, maybe, or discover that an acquaintance had a different last name. She called this 'slippage', and she didn't mind it much. Sometimes, she couldn't even pin down what in the world had changed, as if she were playing a 'spot the difference' game drawn by a too-subtle artist.

A screaming, earth-shattering orgasm, on the other hand, could be quite a different story. Her major transformed from English to chemistry, with a full scholarship thrown in. Changes weren't always positive. After a particularly inspired night with Katie, Genevieve's new world included hostile, divorced parents rather than parents approaching their 30-year wedding anniversary.

Over time, she noticed that the universes she traveled through came in what she thought of as 'clusters'—variations on specific events in her life. Small changes might cycle through different manicures she might have given herself. Bigger changes clustered around significant events—like going to college and choosing a major.

Once Genevieve got together with Katie at a women in science lunch early Junior year, this piece of trivia about her changing world began to feel ominous. Katie was perfect, everything she wanted, and meeting her seemed like the most significant event of Genevieve's life. What if, for the sake of a single orgasm, she woke up to find a reality in which Katie didn't love her, anymore?

The gunman may have taken Katie from her, but Genevieve could barely comprehend a world in which Katie had died. She couldn't imagine it, despite having to live in it. She needed to get out. She masturbated frequently, hoping to wake up in Katie's arms, smelling the sweat of the night before soaked into the bed sheets.

Genevieve discovered a bad habit that held her back. She'd been so afraid of losing Katie that she'd learned to cut off her orgasm, to hold it back and keep it small. She couldn't manage to produce anything powerful enough to really make her travel, especially not when every fantasy and dirty thought had begun to remind her of all she had lost and could not regain.

She needed to let go and come hard enough to get out of this cluster of reality and into a world where Katie hadn't died.

Genevieve went to the store and bought a new butt plug, a big bottle of lube, and a vibrator designed to stimulate both her clit and her G-spot. She returned to her dorm room and stripped. She stared down at her body for a long time, then around at her room. She didn't care if she wound up at a different college, or in another country, or without the autographed collection of concert tickets that currently adorned her wall. She didn't care if she did wind up in a world where she had five hands, or with a sibling she'd never heard of. She needed Katie back.

She couldn't avoid thinking of Katie, so Genevieve embraced the memories, closing her eyes and running her hands slowly down over her breasts the way Katie used to do. A pang shot through her chest and her throat clenched, but Genevieve didn't stop what she was doing.

Her mind rolled back to the first night with Katie, when the giddy laughter that had bubbled up between them had dropped, and they'd stood face to face, trembling with desire. Genevieve remembered biting her lip, unsure of how to cross the bit of space that remained between them in a room that suddenly seemed short of air. Katie took the bold step, yanking Genevieve's shirt off over her head, and then breaking out in a goofy grin that relaxed the tension. They'd tumbled into Genevieve's narrow bed, having fun again, tickling each other and peeling off their clothes. Only once they were naked did the serious mood return.

Katie's forehead had creased in concentration as she'd touched Genevieve, her fingers moving slowly and deliberately, almost studious in her attention to every millimeter of Genevieve's bare flesh.

Tears rolled down Genevieve's cheeks as she remembered, but she lay back slowly on the bed and mimicked Katie's movements that night, trying to discover herself the way her lover had discovered her. She lubed her toys and switched the vibrator on. Genevieve toyed with her nipples and teased her slit open. She pressed a finger against the ring of muscle around her asshole and began to coax it to take her in. She eased the vibrator into her cunt and adjusted it until she found the sweetest spot. Holding the vibrator lightly in place with one hand, she used the other to tease herself with the butt plug, penetrating herself slowly until her ass opened to it. Genevieve gasped and threw back her head at the intensity of sensation. Still not sure it would be enough, she switched the vibrator up a couple notches and played back her memories of Katie on the first night as vividly as she could.

How did Katie look? Slender but strong, every shade of black and brown, large eyes and slim fingers with the nails cut short, muscles visible on the fronts of her thighs, delicate feet with calluses on the sides of her big toes. Genevieve had kissed those calluses, licked every inch of those toes, as Katie giggled and eventually began to moan.

How did Katie feel? Words like velvet and silky didn't seem soft enough. Genevieve remembered the slight tackiness of Katie's skin as they'd both begun to sweat from the heat of holding each other so close and straining together so hard. But underneath that had been an expensive smoothness—she would later learn that Katie enjoyed indulging herself with high-end skin care products. Genevieve had pressed her cheek against Katie's breasts, her stomach, and the feathery, salty-scented tuft of hair between her legs.

How did Katie sound? She'd been loud at first, laughing and filling the cramped room with bold and dirty talk. But Genevieve had kissed her until she'd softened, and her bravado dropped. She'd slipped between Katie's legs and pressed tongue to clit with an infinite patience born of desire and disbelief. Katie's words had turned to sighs, like wind whispering through leaves. When her voice returned, it came deeper, throatier. It originated from low in her belly, and she vocalized her pleasure in little aching throbs that caught in her throat before swelling to a rich moan in the shape of Genevieve's name.

How did Katie smell? Almonds, of course. Salt. Mint. A pungent sweetness that grew ever more powerful as Genevieve licked Katie's labia open and worked one then two then three fingers inside her. And later, when Genevieve had kissed her, Katie had smelled of Genevieve, and of their mingled juices.

How did Katie taste? Her sugared maple lip gloss had concealed the more delicious flavor of her unadorned mouth—a fruity sweetness particular to her. Genevieve had licked the salty caramel tips of Katie's nipples until they turned hard and rough under her tongue. And Katie's cunt held the sharp, succulent mystery of a night-blooming flower.

Genevieve twisted her head to the side and sobbed into the pillow, uncertain by then if she cried from loss or an overload of pleasure. She pushed the vibrator into herself so hard it hurt and slapped the base of the butt plug with her free hand. She came so hard that she didn't have to search for how the world changed.

She could feel it changing, taking hold of the center of her body and radiating outward, stealing her breath as her walls dripped with an uncertain variety of colors and possible objects. Her head pounded as she flinched at every spike of pleasure.

Slowly, Genevieve returned to herself, beeps at regular intervals signaling that her narrow bed now resided in a hospital rather than a dorm room. She waited for her whole self to form, but when she felt nothing from her lower half but vague sensations, she swept her blanket aside and confronted her changed condition for the first time. A catheter sprouted from her insensate lower body. She could not move her toes.

But Genevieve felt no alarm. Without needing to be told, she guessed her victory. In this world, not only did Katie live, but Genevieve was the hero who had protected her, taking the gunman's bullet in her stead.

The echoes of her powerful orgasm still rippled through her body, but the dull result of prodding her clit did not disturb her. If she never came again, then she would never risk returning to the horror of a world without her lover.

Genevieve was still naked when Katie returned home. "Are you awake?" Katie whispered from the doorway of the bedroom. Genevieve's eyes, well-adjusted to the darkness of the room, easily detected the mascara streaks running down her cheeks.

"I'm awake."

"Good." Katie came to the bed and melted into Genevieve's arms. She kissed Genevieve's hairline fiercely. "I want us to be together as equals, not like we owe each other."

"You don't owe me, Katie."

"You don't owe me, either. Let me do this for you."

Genevieve sighed. She hadn't traveled here from another universe just to lose Katie. She'd let Katie touch her, and maybe she could fake an orgasm if that would make Katie happy. Her injury had to mean she was safe, that she wouldn't come at all, and certainly not hard enough to take her away from this. "OK," she breathed.

Katie answered with a kiss that deepened into a wild, full-on grope session. For the first time in years, Katie slid her hand down to Genevieve's waist. Genevieve twitched. This was the transition point between where she had feeling and where she didn't, and the gentle stroking of Katie's fingers burned and scratched one moment, then faded to a ghostly breath the next. She sucked her breath in between her teeth and clamped her eyes shut.

"Sshh," Katie soothed, kissing all over Genevieve's face and down the side of her neck. "Let me touch you."

Genevieve focused on relaxing her breathing, and slowly the raw, quivering sensations around her waist made her upper body writhe. An ache she hadn't known existed began in the interior of her belly. Her hand moved toward her clit in a long-forgotten instinct.

"Good," Katie said. "Can I lift you into your chair and take you to the shower?"

"Why?" Genevieve moaned, frantic and confused.

"I thought hot water would feel good. Besides, I want to clean you up real good to get you ready for all the dirty things I'm going to do to you."

"OK," Genevieve said again.

But once they reached the shower, Katie had more surprises. She pulled off her dress to reveal a lace bikini, through which Genevieve could see her erect nipples. She turned the water on and washed Genevieve with painstaking care and sensuality, covering every part so thoroughly that Genevieve was panting by the time it was through, just from thinking about Katie's fingers gently working her over from forehead to asshole to feet and back.

Cleaning accomplished, Katie rubbed her body all over Genevieve's, and imagination or not, Genevieve was sure she felt flashes of the rough stroking of Katie's lace-covered breasts rubbing her thighs, and maybe even a few moments of the stabbing pleasure of Katie's tongue across her clit.

"You're wet," Katie breathed, in a tone of wonder.

"I'd have come seven times by now if I could," Genevieve said helplessly.

"People say they can still come, even if they don't have sensation," Katie said between licks, reaching her fingers up to tug at Genevieve's lips and probe into her mouth. Genevieve opened for them and gasped when she tasted her own arousal slick and tangy on Katie's hand. Katie continued, working her fingers in and out of Genevieve's mouth. "People say it's different, but it's still an orgasm."

A finger of doubt rippled up Genevieve's confused spinal cord. She didn't want to stop anything or fake anything. Would it be safe to let Katie continue? If she came only in her mind, would that count, as far as the universe was concerned?

Before Genevieve could carry out her thoughts, Katie caught her in a breathless kiss. Steam from the shower heated Genevieve everywhere. Katie draped herself sinuously over Genevieve, pushing one nipple into her lover's mouth and relying on the strength of Genevieve's arms to hold her steady.

Genevieve sucked the nipple and teased Katie's asshole with one fingertip. She didn't expect the powerful shiver that came when Katie scraped her lower teeth over the back of her neck. Katie wriggled in her grasp, freeing her breast and positioning herself so her lips and teeth could reach Genevieve's back. She straddled Genevieve's shower seat, body high enough that Genevieve could dip her head and taste Katie's cunt.

Katie licked and nipped at Genevieve's shoulder blade as if it were her clit, beginning an endless journey from one shoulder blade to the other and back, her teeth pricking and her tongue slipping. She gasped in response to Genevieve's attentions between her thighs, but would not be distracted from her own efforts.

Sensations shooting down Genevieve's back and up her neck became so intense that she eventually had to give way, dropping her head and arching her body up toward her lover's lips, barely remembering to continue using her hands to support Katie's body.

Finally, Katie swung her head up and away from Genevieve, curving her back gracefully, seeming almost like a ballerina performing a lift across Genevieve's shower seat. She was grinning. "How are you feeling?" she asked, and Genevieve could not remember the last time her lover had looked so free.

"Good."

"I'm glad. Are you ready for my next trick?"

"You have another?"

A carefree giggle that Genevieve could not remember hearing since before the night with the gunman. "I have an infinite amount." Katie disappeared for a moment, then returned to the shower flushed, dripping, and smiling. She brandished a thick bit of silicone. "Vibrating butt plug," she said.

"What?"

"They use anal stimulation on men with your condition," Katie said. "To make them ejaculate. Considering how much you used to love it when I played with your ass... I think we should find out what it does to a woman."

"What? Katie!"

"I'm going to feel with my finger first and make sure it's very relaxed back here. I'm watching closely, making sure that this won't hurt you. You can trust me and enjoy this."

Again, an internal stab of arousal pulsed through Genevieve. She'd never felt anything like it, starting in her stomach and traveling, making her experience for the first time all the things she knew intellectually about her sexual organs still functioning.

"I've got three fingers in your ass," Katie whispered. "It's sucking me in. I could fuck you with the largest dildo right now. I wish I'd gotten a big strap-on. Maybe I will. I want to pound your ass.

"But right now, I'm going to lube up the plug and put it in you. It's going to vibrate all through your body. Maybe it'll make your ribcage quiver, or you'll feel it at the bottom of your lungs. Maybe you'll feel a little chatter in your teeth. Whatever you feel, you're going to know it's there. You're going to know that I've stuffed you full of this big, thick plug, and that I'm fucking it in and out of you, and that I'm going to leave it there while I come around to the front and rub my clit into your face until I come so hard..."

Genevieve did feel it in her teeth and in her ribcage and in her lungs. She even felt it in her fingertips and her earlobes. She could swear she could feel vibration in her whole body, just like Katie said. She couldn't help letting it shake her. And when Katie followed through with her promise and thrust her cunt into Genevieve's face, Genevieve opened her mouth and tasted her and gasped brokenly against her slit as a strange, slow spasm traveled her body, bringing pleasure to every muscle it touched. "I love you," Katie said in a voice like hot amber honey.

"No," Genevieve whispered, and tried to cling to Katie, but she could not stop the world from shifting.

It took days for Genevieve to recover from the shock of feeling her feet. Every twitch of her toe felt painful. She could not break the habit of dismissing itching as a phantom sensation. She walked once around the small apartment where she woke up, then lay on the twin bed and cried.

She had known the moment she'd opened her eyes that Katie did not live in this place. No smell of almonds. No strands of dark hair across the pillows. No bottle of hand lotion on the night stand.

In this world, Genevieve had a job and friends who went to happy hour and no love interest she could discover. She had a spine that communicated fully with every part of her body as well as with her brain. She studied her filing cabinet and read her e-mail with all the concentration of the archaeologists who deciphered the Code of Hammurabi. She found a LiveJournal account where she occasionally wrote about her memories of Katie. Had Katie died here, too?

She went to work for a few days and hung out with these strange new friends before she got up the courage to look for Katie. Her love turned out to be only a few searches away. Genevieve found Katie's address and, the next day, showed up on her doorstep and rang the bell.

There was a long pause, and then the door swung open. From her wheelchair, Katie looked up at Genevieve with a mixture of wonder and disbelief. "You said you wouldn't be back," she whispered.

In what universe could she ever have left Katie? Genevieve clenched her jaw to hold back the exclamations that would have confused this version of Katie. Genevieve took a moment to admire the definition and strength of Katie's arms, and the way she managed to use that almond-scented oil to tame her black hair out of escaping with even a single flyaway. She couldn't resist the temptation of this angle, which afforded a view straight down Katie's cleavage.

When the silence stretched a moment, Katie talked into it, her words coming thick and fast. "I can't tell you how many times I wished I'd let you touch me. I couldn't believe you still found me attractive, that you still wanted me. It was like I owed you, and I couldn't take any pleasure from you in return for anything."

"I understand. Really, I do."

Katie shook her head. "I'm so sorry. I see now how hard that must have been for you. You just wanted us to be normal with each other, equal lovers. I couldn't do that then. I didn't see what you could possibly do for me."

Genevieve stared for a moment, then a slow smile spread over her face. "I actually have a lot of ideas about what I could do for you."

Katie blinked. Genevieve had to remind herself that this version of Katie hadn't been with her for a long time, and wasn't used to the easy innuendo that grows up between lovers. "I don't mean to freak you out," Genevieve said. "I just missed you."

Katie cleared her throat. "Do you want to come in for some tea? Just talk, maybe?"

Genevieve nodded. She might not be able to stay in this universe, either, but as long as she found Katie somewhere, she trusted that all would be repaired.

So Quite New A Thing
R. Ann Sawyer

I stood just behind Elaine, watching as she turned her head from side to side, studying the way the earrings looked in her lobes. I'd bought the silver dangles on a business trip. I claimed that I'd bought them for me, but I doubted that either of us believed me. I never wore earrings like this, but they suited Elaine perfectly. It was all part of the quiet, ongoing flirtation that we'd been carrying on for the past decade.

Early on, it had been somewhat regretful; we'd been burning for each other, but too many things got in the way. Eventually, it just seemed foolish to talk about it; why ruin our friendship? Besides, she'd never seemed interested in me—not really. Her girlfriends were always much more put together than me, the sort of women who made online videos about makeup and hair styles—who ran half-marathons and still looked pretty at the end. I ran full marathons, and sweated like a pig while I was doing it.

I knew what she was thinking as she studied the earrings so carefully; the furrow between her brows as she wondered how these would look in the office; the slight narrowing of the eyes as she considered how they would brush against her neck as she accepted a drink from a cutie at a bar. I'd have told her, if she would have asked; they looked lovely on her, just ghosting against her neck enough to make them sparkle and sway. On me, they'd looked like peacock feathers on a chicken; on Elaine, as so many things did, they looked like perfection. "They are gorgeous, Meg," she said. "Are you really sure you want to give them up?"

I tried to make a face like I was unsure, mostly just to keep watching her move. She glanced up at my reflection, our eyes meeting in the mirror, and I felt the lightning bolt zing that I'd never learned to ignore. In the beginning, I'd thought she'd felt it too. But for the past year, neither of us had been seeing anyone seriously, and she still ducked away from me if I watched her too long. Maybe it was all in my imagination.

Something in my expression made her smile. "What is it?" she asked.

"Nothing," I said. "They suit you." I wanted her throat under my lips and my teeth. I wanted her breasts under my hands. I wanted her body pressed into mine as she sighed into release. But, yeah... it wasn't going to happen. I watched her in the mirror as she turned her eyes back to her own reflection—and then I watched as my reflection moved toward hers. I was rooted in place, not moving a muscle, but my reflection moved closer to Elaine's, bending over her, lips suddenly caressing over the curve of her neck, settling, for a moment, in the crease of her shoulder, and then sliding back, a secret smile on my mirror-face. I felt my eyes widen and my cheeks flush, and I was a hot minute away from shifting uncomfortably in my plain-Jane cotton panties.

Mirror-Elaine seemed thrilled with these proceedings, her own mouth spreading into a smile as her head dropped back onto my shoulder, her lips moving, shaping words I couldn't hear. My Elaine was silent, fidgeting with the earrings, but there was no hint that she was seeing anything out of the ordinary. I blinked hard, waiting for the fantasy to end, for reality to reassert itself— but no. I watched my hand reach up and cup Elaine's breast, fingers dusting over her nipple, making her mouth form a perfect O for a moment. I watched her turn to kiss me. I couldn't breathe. I couldn't think.

"Okay," Elaine said, still studying as her reflection tilted its head down, giving my mouth more access to the soft planes of her throat. "If you really don't want them, Meg, I'll definitely take them off your hands."

My throat was parched. My clit was swelling, aching, my body drenching itself in hopeless moisture. "Sure," I managed. "They look better on you, anyway."

"Are you okay? You look like you saw a ghost."

In the mirror, I watched as Elaine turned her mouth up to me, and I captured it, possessed it. No, not a ghost. Just a fantasy. A dream I'd never let myself dream. Not while I was awake, anyway. I felt the small sound of yearning building inside of me, and I shoved it away. Far, far away. What was the point? It was better to have Elaine as a friend than to not have her. Surely if my feelings were reciprocated, she would have made a move by now; I wasn't subtle about my interest.

So I'd made myself stop thinking about her so much. I'd dated a bunch of other women, waiting for someone who enraptured me like she did. No dice, but I'd managed to mostly put it out of my mind. Until I experienced some sort of mental break brought on by staring at my best friend's neck too much. Or something.

I could almost hear the soft sounds of appreciation coming from Elaine's throat as I teased her nipples and eased my tongue past her soft lips. We'd kissed once before, when she was very, very drunk. I'd never been sure if she actually remembered. How could you ask? "Hey, remember the night you were heartbroken because the love of your life left you for a twenty-year-old, yogi vegetarian, and we did vodka shots until the sun came up, and then you French kissed me? No? Oh. Well, it was good for me, anyway." Because that wouldn't be awkward.

"Meg?" She was looking up into the mirror. At where my reflection would be, if it wasn't doing all the things that I wished I could.

"Yeah. I'm okay." God, she'd turned now, kissing me full on, and I went down on my knees between her legs. There was an urgency building between us; she had her hands on either side of my face, and I was grasping at her, my hands moving frantically over her back, crushing her against me. My hand slipped between us, rubbing at the seam of her pants—God, why hadn't she worn a skirt; she looked so good in skirts, why not today of all days?— and her head dropped back, her eyes slipping closed, her teeth closed over her lower lip. I was at her throat again, teeth this time, nipping softly at that exposed flesh—at the sweet, soft skin. I could feel the vibration of her sound under me, even if I couldn't hear it.

"Meg?" My Elaine was standing now, moving in front of me, and I couldn't look over her shoulder to see what was happening. "You look like you're having a seizure."

I forced myself to focus on her face. "I'm sorry. I'm fine. Just—a headache. All of a sudden."

Her brow furrowed, her eyes full of concern. "Do you need to lie down? Can I get you anything?"

"No—no, just go." Just go and let me watch. "I'll be fine. I'm fine."

She stepped aside, and the mirror was just a mirror again. The fantasy broke, and the headache came for real, splashing pain over me in droplets. I swayed on my feet, and she caught me, easing me down into the chair. "What can I do?" she asked again.

"Water," I said. "Ibuprofen."

She knew my apartment as well as she knew her own, and she steadied me on the small vanity stool for just a moment before heading to my bathroom. I stared at the mirror, willing the vision to return. Nothing. I leaned forward, as if I could peer down into the space between the glass and the reflection, and the cool smoothness felt like it gave just a bit with my forehead, as if enough pressure would let me fall through into that space where I kissed Elaine, and she reached out for me.

"Here," she said, helping me upright again, not knowing that she was shattering a dream into tiny fragments. She pressed a glass into my hand, two tablets into my mouth, and then her strong, slender fingers wove into my hair as I took the pills that wouldn't change anything. You can't medicate away lust. God knew I'd tried.

"Relax," she said, stepping closer to me. She spread her legs just a bit and stood, one on either side of my knees, pulling my head softly forward, until my forehead rested against her smooth, strong, stomach. She worked the muscles of my shoulders and neck, her fingers digging into tension she'd created a decade ago. I kept all the gasps and whimpers inside.

Was that a touch of desire in her hands? Did she trace her fingers down my spine for just a half a second on that down-stroke? Did her nails linger in my hair for just a moment? Was that sound out loud?

The torture didn't stop. "Is that helping?" she asked. "Any better at all?"

The fantasy was gone. So was the headache, under her careful fingers, but it had been replaced by a low, slow ache in the depths of my belly that I wasn't going to be able to solve with her here. "A little. I should lie down. I feel dizzy."

I looked up as she caught her lip in her teeth. "Maybe you need a doctor."

"I'm fine," I said, and I stood up to prove my point. I thought she'd fall back from me—step away. She didn't. She held perfectly still. Maybe I could have fit a piece of paper between us. Maybe. She was smaller than me—not a lot, but just enough that she had to tilt her head back, just a hair, to meet my eyes. Her hands had fallen away from my hair as I stood, and now they hovered awkwardly, a little bit away from her body and mine. And then, slowly, they closed in and settled on my hips. I watched her lips move through several words that she didn't say, before finally stilling.

"Hi," she said. "Um."

"Hi." My voice was weird, and breathy, and strange. If she were anyone else, I'd think she was begging me to kiss her, but Elaine? My Elaine? Still, when was I ever going to be this close to her again? My hand came up to one of her brown curls. I'd always wanted to tangle my hand in them, to see if she fit into my palm quite as well as I thought she might. There was no other time when I'd get to try. She pressed into my hand like a kitten, and yes, she even sighed sweetly at the pressure.

I leaned down slowly, giving her all the time in the world to step away, to say no, to change her mind. She didn't move, didn't run. She trembled, gently, under my hand, but I had a crazy idea that it was with eagerness, rather than disgust. And when my lips brushed hers, I felt the motion of the planet underneath me and the stars above me. I felt the gush of warmth in my pants. I felt my nipples, so hard and sharp and aching that I thought they might tear through my shirt.

I wanted to rip her apart and crawl inside, but I kept my kisses light and soft. It was her who let out a groan, swollen with need; who clenched her hands into fists in the small of my back and pressed her curves into mine, complete and whole. A wall inside me tore down. We were inches from my bed, and it was a moment's work to tip us down onto its soft surface. We landed side by side, and she was already fumbling with the zipper of her jeans. I went after the buttons on her shirt, pleased with myself for having enough control to ease each and every tiny button through its tiny buttonhole, and not just doing my best to rip the thing off of her. My pants and t-shirt followed hers. And then we laid there, a slow moment in the midst of the frenzy. My hand traced the curve of her hip down onto her thigh, then slid back up onto the soft swell of her stomach. She held still, letting me drink her in, watching me carefully.

"Are you—" I started.

She smelled my doubt in the air. "You stopped kissing me," she said. "You should fix that." And she reached out and pinched my left nipple harder than I would have said I liked, but the searing twist of it made me gasp and arch into the air for a moment.

I caught her mouth with mine, just to find a way to breathe, and she whimpered against me as my fingers traced knots and whorls down her soft, smooth skin. As they brushed over the top of her trimmed-down thatch of dark hair, she parted her thighs for me, sighing into my mouth as my forefinger slipped down into that shockingly wet slit. She went silent and still as I traced gently around her clit, never quite making full contact, circling. Dancing down to where she opened to me, almost sliding into her, then coming back up to circle.

She rolled back onto her back, spreading her thighs to give me total access to her. Only her hips moved, arching in a gentle rhythm to the motion of my caresses. My mouth, possessed, fell to work on her nipples, teasing them softly between my teeth, suckling at them, filling my hands with them. Her mouth opened wide as her back bent underneath me, and I slid my fingers softly inside of her, moving with her own rhythm, gently.

Two fingers inside of her, a third putting soft pressure on her ass, and she was making a sound: a soft, low, unbroken keening that carried on and on. Her head tossed on my pillow, and her hips shuddered more than thrust. As she peaked, she got quieter, but her motions were almost violent, thrashing as she convulsed and squeezed around my fingers, gasping for air. I let her come and come, and when she started to come back to earth, I moved inside her again until she squeezed her thighs tight over my hand. "I'm good," she whispered, breathless. "I'm good for now."

The aftershocks hadn't even fully stopped before she pushed me over onto my back. "You don't have to—" I started. "Meg," she said, in the same exasperated tone she used on her cat when he'd gotten into her knitting, "knock it the fuck off, or I seriously will stop."

Never let it be said that I couldn't follow orders. I descended into pleasure as she left a trail of hot kisses down my stomach, nudging my knees apart with hers. I couldn't breathe, couldn't think. Elaine was kissing me. My Elaine. And not in some crazy mirror fantasy.

And then she looked up to give me one last, sweet smile before her tongue wrapped around my clit, and my mind stopped thinking, concentrated instead on feeling her strong hands clenching around my thighs and her tongue exploding waves of pleasure through me. I wasn't quiet. I moaned and cried out and arched my back, but she stayed latched to me, never wavering in the smooth, delicate motion of her tongue. And when she slid her fingers inside of me, the world ended while I screamed my pleasure out to anyone on the block who cared to listen.

When I could think again, she was cuddled into me, soft and warm. I wrapped my arm tightly around her shoulders, luxuriating in the weight of her leg over my hips. "Why tonight?" I said.

It seemed the only question worth asking.

I could feel her smile in the curve of her back. "It just looked like we were having so much fun in the mirror. I had to give it a shot."

Reflections
Kate Dominic

Like everyone else in my family, I'd been given the requisite book on the day of my birth. My parents, aunts, uncles, distant elder cousins, and damn near every other one of my self-described 'incredibly gifted' relatives had thrown their opinions into the selection of photos in the book of bedtime stories that would be read to me, and when I was able, that I'd read to myself every night for the rest of my life. The faces in the photos were of those the elders expected I'd be most likely to connect with when I grew old enough and skilled enough to 'communicate' with what we referred to as 'distant family and friends.'

The faces in my book were, as far as I could tell, randomly drawn from portraits, sculptures, meticulously preserved artifacts, and every other imaginable type of art residing in the world class museum, excuse me, 'private art gallery' in the ancient family estate back in Ireland. We're talking everything from WWII black and white photos to oil paintings of beautifully-gowned Renaissance ladies with powdered bosoms to half-naked bull jumpers dancing around a 3,000 year old piece of Mediterranean pottery.

I grew up reading the stories of the people in the photos, getting to know them and the worlds in which they lived. At the age of 25, and in the midst of dealing with the relatives' reactions to my steampunk phase, I discovered that not only did the rest of my crazy family believe the stories in our books were true, they really expected me to use the artwork as portals to visit the people in the pictures, and vice versa. Everybody in the family—on both sides of the artwork—apparently did; time and space didn't mean much when it came time for the annual May Day gathering at the family estate.

The castle was old and gray and huge, with three stories (not counting the turrets) of living space stuffed to the gills with insane, albeit beautifully-preserved artwork. Every day after my walks in the lush, quiet grounds outside, I damn near broke out in hives just coming back in the door. It wasn't that I didn't appreciate the family 'gift' of portal traveling. But not once in the hours leading up to tonight's May Day festivities had I felt so much as a twinge of—well, anything—when I approached the original pieces that were, theoretically, my doors to connect with the people shown therein.

I'd had my book and the castle's annotated floor plan in hand, to be sure I was looking at the right pieces. I'd checked out every single one, giving special attention to ones associated with the pictures I'd always liked best, especially now that I was seeing the entire works of art, boobs and pussies and all, not just the sanitized versions in my story book. Thank gods the photos in my book had only been cropped; I'd seen one cousin's book where they'd PhotoShopped in fig leaves!

I'd been treated to a room full of Greek goddesses sculpted from glowing white marble, their chitons draped gracefully to reveal firm, perfect breasts. A life-sized oil painting showed two medieval peasant women clearing dinner from a noble's table, their loose shifts falling off their shoulders to reveal heavy breasts with well-suckled nipples—true 'nurses', I realized, when I saw the wet spot on the well-worn, and no doubt very soft, linen covering one woman's full, dark nipples. It wasn't that I didn't appreciate a bare-breasted lassie in or out of any kind of attire. My pussy got so wet I could help squeezing my legs together each time I made the rounds to 'my' artwork. But there was no single time or face that called out to me. No matter how many times I dutifully checked and rechecked, my response was the same. Zero. Zip. Nada.

The only thing I felt when I returned from my afternoon walk was a headache that had me once again slapping on sunglasses the moment I stepped back indoors. A door that had previously been closed was opened across from the main entrance. I staggered into the—parlor, apparently—to sit down, and collapsed into a cream silk chair, letting my purse fall onto a marble-topped coffee table. Even the three glasses of wine I gulped at the suggestion of a disgustingly cheerful distant cousin didn't scratch the surface of my pounding headache. And that was when I realized that the portal visiting had started. Throughout the castle, the air vibrated with a cacophony of contemporary voices, languages, and music, mixing with sounds from way too many other eras. And over it all was the smell of everything from body odor to tea and liquor, and roasting things I couldn't identify, and didn't want to think too much about. And over it all, the overwhelming perfume of too-much patchouli.

All the place needed was a Cheshire cat and someone yelling "Off with her head!" Which at this point, I wasn't sure I would have minded. I was reserving judgment on whether or not mushrooms were involved in the cooking. Holy fuck—this was my heritage?

I watched my sister walk dreamy-eyed into a photo of a cavalier, and was shocked to discover I 'saw' her walking hand-in-hand with him off screen. Okay, so maybe I had some of the family gift. Or maybe it was just the May Day vibes letting everyone see.

I stared in shock as a gorgeous young man I assumed was some sort of distant relative hurried, naked, up to a life-sized statue of a wrestler and slathered lube on the enormous marble erection. Then he turned around, held his cheeks open, and grinning ecstatically, backed his ass up onto the glistening hard-on. At his cry of "Mon ami, je retourne!" the statue's eyes closed in bliss, and the young man faded into the stone.

It didn't take me long to realize that all the visitors, whether coming or going, were traveling to connect with lovers. And by lunch time, I knew a helluva lot of people were making multiple trips. Fancy cravats were askew by the third or fourth booty call, and several of the women had taken to leaving their stays unlaced as they hurried from one piece of art to another. One disheveled 30-something woman in a kirtle hurried out of a 14th century triptych of St. Ursula. The woman's bodice was open, one well-sucked, still-damp nipple exposed, and her face flushed with sex. She ran up to a man wearing a flowing, Renaissance shirt and hose, who started untying his codpiece as soon as he saw her.

I caught something along the lines of "Oh, there you are, dear! Come quickly, Marta is pregnant, so she can't come through the portal, but she so wants to fuck us!" At least that's what I thought they said. I couldn't tell for sure. They were speaking in what I thought was old German. She tugged the man toward the picture she'd just exited. He laughed, kissed her soundly, and with his erection leading the way, they went hand-in-hand back into the painting of the 'virgins.'

I smiled despite my headache, and once again got up to retrace my steps to every one of the pictures in my book. They were exclusively women, I realized, and all very attractive. Not necessarily beautiful, though some were. But they were all hot and sexy in their own unique ways. Looking at every one of their full-sized depictions made my pussy hum. Obviously, the book was accurate in that sense.

But no one 'spoke' to me. I made it through dinner in what was apparently the first of three nights of riotously indulgent feasting. Lots of oysters and fortifying wine. And as people went off for their evening assignations, I tucked my book in my purse and snuck off upstairs in search of some peace and quiet.

Most of the rooms were occupied with orgiastic twosomes, threesomes, or more, and the spaces that were empty for now were as cluttered with art as the rest of the house; I had no idea who might pop in through a painting at any time. On the third floor, when I turned the corner at the end of a long maze of halls, the noise finally started to abate. A short flight of stairs with only one huge, fucking painting—this of a woman, from the back, riding her horse—led up to an open turret door. Gold light spilled out into the hall. But there were no clothes strewn in the doorway, and no sounds or smells of sex wafting out into the hall.

I walked in the door—into quiet. Blessed, blessed quiet. The room was more a suite than just a bedroom. A high, canopied bed with thick, red velvet covers and gold bed curtains rested against the far wall. The curtains were tied back with heavy silk cords, and the bed was piled high with pillows in red velvet shams and gold brocade. A single, old-fashioned, chemise-type nightgown was folded at the foot of the bed.

I took off my sunglasses and stuffed them in my purse. A cheerful fire burned in a plain marble fireplace to the far side of the bed, and soft light from the bedside lamps glowed on the overstuffed cream-silk chairs and sofa in the sitting area, the subtly shaded cream wallpaper, and plush carpet just a shade lighter. Heavy gold curtains shot through with red were drawn tightly closed over the single window to the near side of the bed. In the center of the sitting area, on a lush red accent rug, a mahogany coffee table with a crisp white linen tablecloth held a silver ice bucket chilling an unopened bottle of champagne, two crystal glasses, two place settings of china and silver, and a tray with an assortment of cheeses and fresh fruit.

There was not one fucking picture. No sculptures. No carvings or castings of any living being. The only thing hanging on the walls anywhere in the room was the huge, old mirror over the sofa, its glass clouded with a patina of age. All that showed within the heavy wooden frame was me in my usual uniform of black leggings and black bustier, my long, dark hair twisted up into chopsticks, and my seriously relieved grin.

A final look into the hall told me no one was out there. The sounds of revelry were only a distant hum. I closed the door and locked it. The lock was loose, but I figured it would hold enough to give me warning if anyone tried to invade. I tossed my purse on the table, sank down onto a chair, and took off my boots. Finally—finally!—the space around me was quiet! I popped the top on the champagne and leaned back in the inordinately comfy chair with a glass of bubbly and a plate of strawberries and brie. With each delicious sip and nibble, I let the calm seep into my bones.

Fuck, I was tired. On the one hand, I was surprised that none of the pictures had opened to me. After a lifetime of reading their lives as bedtime stories, I felt like I knew them all. And now that I understood how the lust could factor in, I had to admit I was seeing them all in a different light. Maybe tomorrow, I'd try it all again. After I got some fucking sleep.

By the end of the first glass, I was relaxed, and my headache was gone. I poured a second glass and took out my book, sipping slowly as I once more visited the people in my bedtime stories. I didn't bother reading. I knew all the stories by heart. I just flipped through the pages, wishing hot, sexy dreams to the familiar faces, wherever they were and whatever they were doing this May Day. I was yawning, so I tucked my book back in my purse, walked over to the bed, and dimmed the lamp to no more than a candle's glow. I stripped naked, pulled the chopsticks from my hair, and started to get into bed.

Shit. I glanced back at the door. I didn't trust that stupid lock, and God only knew who might come carousing in the door tonight. I hated sleeping in clothes, but I was so not up to defending my space naked. I picked up the nightgown. It was incredibly soft and so girly. Not my usual attire by any stretch of the imagination. But it was there, and I was exhausted. I pulled it on, shivering as the well-washed linen slid down over my body like a lover's hand. Each time I moved my shoulders, my nipples got harder. When I turned to look at myself in the mirror, I had to admit I looked hot in a lusty, medieval wench kind of way. The top of the chemise fell open, revealing a swell of cleavage I usually only saw above black leather. My pebbled nipples poked into the soft, white fabric draping over me in a way that drew my eyes like lasers to my breasts, and to the curves and shadows of my hips.

I loved looking at myself in candlelight, and there was a big, fat, triple-wicked candle on the nightstand, along with a pack of matches. I lit the candle, turned off the lamp, and drew back the covers. Then I climbed into bed and slid between the sinfully delicious sheets. I leaned back against the pillows, watching my reflection in the mirror as I made myself comfortable.

The sheets felt as good on my skin as the nightgown did on my nipples. It wasn't long before my fingers were roaming, and my pussy was wet. Between that and a day of being around literally eons' worth of randy people and interportal fucking, I wished my vibrator was handy. But I was so not going to leave my sanctuary for a dorm-style room with a bunch of lust-crazed hetero chicks.

The candlelight danced in the mirror, surprisingly bright. I kicked back the covers and rucked up the end of my nightgown, smiling as the juice from my pussy made my labia glisten. I circled my clit, shivering as I watched it stiffen.

I loved masturbating in front of a mirror. I couldn't see my pussy from that angle, except as a reflection, but the visuals of my fingers moving in and over my pussy always made me come so much harder. I wet my fingers in my slit, shivering with anticipation, toying with my clit, watching my reflection mirror my movements.

I rubbed in circles until my legs trembled. I was so close, I could have come right then, but I was feeling greedy. I always felt greedy when I masturbated in front of the mirror. I wanted more, and I wanted it to last longer. I slid my middle finger down my slit, dipping inside, gliding on my juices. Two fingers. Three. Pressing up hard until I shivered and moaned, watching myself do the things I was feeling. In the glass, the flame from the candle danced in the evening breeze.

My hand stilled. The window was closed. There was no breeze in the room. A chill raced through me as I realized the fingers in the mirror were still pumping, even though mine weren't.

Oh, please! My reflection's hand slowed to the patient, steady rocking that always brought me such a good come. The rocking that so often made my pussy squirt. *Don't stop now. We need to come!* A low chuckle whispered through the room. *At least I need to come! If you don't want to, turn away from the mirror, so I can.*

I rocked my hand. I couldn't help it. It felt so good, and I—or she, or whoever the hell was in the mirror—looked so hot. The woman's legs were spread, her slick, shiny fingers buried deep between her juicy, pink folds.

As soon as my hand moved, she laughed and put her thumb on her clit. It felt like I was being drawn by a magnet as I moaned and did the same. Our hands rocked, our thumbs circled. At the same moment, we reached down and spread our pussy lips so we could see better. And we laughed.

Most of the gifted can only see their portal companions come alive at the gathering. But you and I both know we've done this before. We can do it every damn day of the year if we want. But the May Day gathering gives us the ability to travel through the portals to touch. Our fingers rocked deep. Then the voice in my head changed to a low, seductive purr. *Do you want to come over and fuck yourself, love?*

My mouth moved all on its own, mimicking hers like I was lip-synching. The smile felt like it was mine, though, or at least mine as much as hers. That having sex with myself would be mind-blowing hot was pretty much a no-brainer. But as I tensed to move, I blurted out, "Will we still be able to watch?"

We laughed, and my hand moved—the one that wasn't still rocking in her/our pussy—to mimic the come hither curl of her other finger.

For these three days, so long as we stay in the mirror, every motion we make will be reflected. We'll see and feel every sensation from both sides, giving and receiving. The only difference will be that you'll be the only one coming through the mirror.

We were still speaking as we slid our hands free. I turned to blow out the candle.

Don't, she said sharply. *This is a very old mirror. Time can move differently here. We need the candles to tell us when it's time for you to go back.*

I frowned and looked at the candle. I had the proper, modern girl's appreciation for the fire hazards related to flames inside a building.

It's safe.

Well, when I looked at the setup, I had to admit, it probably was. There was nothing flammable close to the candle, and the big metal holder with its big glass globe looked large enough and sturdy enough to handle pretty much anything the wax did. Besides, I had the feeling that such things were taken care of in this particular castle.

I stood up and stretched, my nightgown falling back into place. I grinned as my reflection's did the same. Then I walked slowly to the mirror, letting my hips sway, watching my breasts move seductively beneath the linen as I walked toward the sofa. I paused at the coffee table, taking time to eat a slice of orange and a nibble of cheese, watching my reflection nibble food—I couldn't see specifically what—from the matching table in her room. Then I untied the top of my gown and took out one breast, toying with the nipple until it stood out stiff and hard. I bit the tip off a strawberry and rubbed it over my nipple, licking my lips as I did, watching her do the same, wondering what my breasts, and hers, would taste like when we licked the bright red juice back off. I ate the rest of the strawberry and dropped the top on my empty plate. Then I climbed up onto the sofa.

My toes curled into the cushions, my fingers sinking deep into the heavy padding on the back. The creamy silk was soft and stimulating. I straightened—we straightened—keeping one hand down for balance, our eyes soft and hungry as we licked our lips. The magnetic tractor-beam feeling was really strong now. I swung up my leg and lifted my free hand to the glass. And this time, only I moved.

The glass was cool and clear, like water. As my hand passed in, I heard someone knocking on the door behind me—knocking and rattling the knob. The door opened, and I heard my great-aunt's voice say, "Oh, shit!"

Then I was through the water, through the mirror. I stopped in stunned surprise as I saw my reflection standing there directly in front of me, in the flesh. Her hands were on her hips, in the same 'unladylike' way my mother was always bitching at me about.

We weren't on a sofa. My toes curled into the smooth, well-worn wood of a sturdy table. When I turned back to the mirror, I realized the sofa didn't show beneath the bottom of the mirror. I could still see my room, but the people moving in there—my elderly aunt, my loudmouthed sister, and a couple of women I'd seen in passing—were waving their hands and pointing at the mirror, but it was more like I was seeing them through a window rather than a mirror. One of them pointed to the candle.

My great-aunt sighed and looked directly at me, holding up three fingers as she mouthed the words "Three days!"

My reflection laughed and drew the curtains over the mirror—curtains I realized weren't on my side of the glass. "If you don't return on the third day," she said, "you're stuck here for good. Same as with all the other 'artwork.'" She took my hand and turned me to face her.

Our movements weren't in sync anymore. I was still looking at a direct reflection rather than seeing the usual left-to-right differences that happened when I was facing a person in real life, or whatever real life was on the other side of the mirror. But the feel of my reflection's fingers was what I noticed most. Her hand was warm and soft, and when I squeezed, I felt both sides of the touch.

"Wow," I said.

"Yes, wow," she smiled. Her voice sounded like mine did on my voicemail recording, but she had an accent that reminded me vaguely of my college Chaucer prof's when she read excerpts from the Canterbury Tales.

The light was different, too. We stepped down off the table, and my reflection lit more candles. Those, and the flames from the fire, were the only light. The air smelled different, too, fresher in a wild, outdoorsy way, yet heavy with people—wood smoke and cooked meat, dried herbs and the not-unpleasant sweat of someone who ate different foods than I did. The sounds of distant laughter and drums vibrated through the walls. I glanced at the door. It was locked with a heavy bolt rather than the modern keyed lock I'd turned—a lock that apparently hadn't kept anyone out. This bolt was sturdier. I sighed. The door, too, was beyond the field of the mirror."Where am I?"

"In your room." She shrugged. "This same room, on the family estate. The difference is when. It's 1720." She smiled and pulled me further into the room. "That's the first question portal travelers usually ask."

My face must have look as astonished as I felt. "This is my first time."

"Oh, really!" She laughed and leaned forward, brushing her lips lightly over mine. My pussy walls clenched so hard, I almost came. My reflection laughed and let me see her shiver, and she kept my hand in hers."I'm being guarded in here to protect my virginity. I'm bound for marriage to an intelligent, good-natured, and extremely beautiful man who has no more interest in women than I have in men. I'll be retiring to his estate right after the wedding, where, a few months later, I will become a mother— to my idiot sister's child. She's been a recluse while her husband is away at the wars. Recluse, hah! She has no idea who the father is."

She laughed and tossed back her hair. "The child's true parentage is of no matter. My husband will have his heir—and can thus retire with his hunting companions. My father will have the joined estates he covets." She ran her finger down the front of her night dress, opening the soft linen front further, exposing more of the full swell of her breasts. "I will have as many lady friends as houseguests as I wish."

God, did my boobs heave like that when I was flirting? Her "we're identical" tumbled out at the same time as my "I hope so! It's so hot—I want to lick everywhere your finger goes."

She laughed and circled her palm over her nipple. "You will," she grinned. "The wedding contract calls for me to be returned here for the first three days of every May, in respect of my family's traditions." Her fingers moved whisper-soft over my shoulder. We shuddered at the sensations. "Father agrees that would be best, so as not to draw attention to our family's somewhat unique traditions."

She leaned toward me, her mouth so close we were sharing breath. We were the same height, of course. With her hair hanging loose, her curls floated down over her breasts.

She lifted a lock of my hair, trailing it along the side of my neck and down over the swell of my breast. I trembled with each brush on my skin, my pussy clenching at her instinctive copycat response.

"Our time is precious," she said, and kissed me.

It was the most mind blowing kiss of my life. I felt both sides, hers, mine, ours, every twitch of her lips, every long slow swipe of her tongue. I felt her tasting the wet heat of my mouth and the strawberry I'd eaten. Finally, she leaned back, panting.

"You first," she said, and slid the linen off my shoulder.

The sensation of her mouth on my breast and my nipple on her tongue had small, constant, mini orgasms rolling through me. The sensations traveled back and forth, tongue to nipple, nipple to tongue, as she licked and kissed and sucked. Then I opened the front of her chemise and took her breast in my mouth, holding it to my lips and kneading deep into her flesh as she'd done to me. I suckled her exactly as she'd done, rhythmically drawing her nipple out over my tongue, stretching it, massaging it between my tongue and the roof of my mouth.

My pussy was quaking, desperate for her fingers. I squeezed my legs together, relishing the pressure, knowing even before she whispered "not yet" that these first hours together were purely for developing intimacy, getting closer, cementing the bond growing between us with sensation.

We kissed and suckled each other's breasts until our lips were swollen, and still reached hungrily for more. Then we pulled off our chemises and lay down side by side on the bed, kissing. Her head was toward the foot of the bed, mine toward the head. We slid apart, just enough to meet lips to nipples. Our nipples were tender; our lips were, too. Still we clasped each other's breasts, opened out mouths, and hungrily latched on.

It was beyond exquisite, almost beyond bearing. Our nipples were so tender, even the lightest licks caused us to tremble and whimper, and lean into the warm, wet suction waiting to nurse sensations through our nipples again.

"More," she whispered, as I slid further down. I rolled on my back, opening my legs to her face as she rolled up and over me, her knees straddling my ears. Her pussy looked just like mine always had in the mirror, swollen pink and wet and hungry. But up this close, I could smell our musk. Her crotch was soaked. Mine was, too. We reached up, holding each other's labia open, drinking in the scents of our pussies. She lowered her face and pussy to me as I lifted mine to her.

Salty, tangy. Mine! I swirled my tongue into her open folds, crying out as her tongue vibrated against me. We circled our clits, licked and laved and sucked, sliding our tongues soft and wet and lusciously questing through our slits, darting in and out of our pussies in a perfectly choreographed dance, sweating and moaning and trembling.

The first big orgasm exploded through us, thunder and lightning and a wild screaming frenzy of sensation and squirting pussies. We licked and sucked until our clits couldn't stand to be touched anymore. Then we sank our fingers into our pussies, gliding on oceans of juice until our probing fingers found out hidden sweet spots. We pressed and rocked, did it over and over, without stopping, until the orgasm built again. The next climax shook us to our bones, our breath coming out in high, keening cries until we could barely breathe.

We spent all that night and the next two days in our room. We dressed each morning in time for the maid, who smiled but asked no questions, to bring us warm water and towels and clean shifts, and for her to empty the chamber pots from behind the screen at the far end of the room, something else beyond the range of the mirror.

Then we were naked on the soft linen sheets again. We took each other on the chair, taking turns kneeling between each other's wide-spread legs, pulling hips to the edge of the seat, then kneeling in front and suckling each other's breasts, going lower and eating each other's pussies until we screamed. We lay on the dining table and licked berry juice from our nipples and ate sweet cream from our clits. We languished on piles of pillows while we talked and rocked our hands knuckles deep inside each other until our pussies trembled and gushed and we squealed in ecstasy. Then we slept and woke and did it all over again, sharing our exquisitely tender breasts and fingering our almost overly sensitized pussies until we keened in mindless ecstasy.

Each time we woke, and each time we orgasmed, we looked at the time candle on this side of the mirror, watching it slowly burn lower. We didn't go near the table by the mirror, lest we accidentally fall through. And on the third day, as the candle burned low in its glass, I lay on top of her, our breasts touching, our nipples stiff and throbbing from the gentle friction of our rocking. We set lips and tongues to our clits, slid the fingers of one hand deep into our creaming pussies, and dipping gobs of soothing, lavender-scented cream on the fingers of our other hands, slid one, then two, then three fingers up our virgin anuses, and fucked our pussies and bottoms until an orgasm beyond sanity quaked, shrieking, through our bodies. We howled until our throats hurt, then we stilled our hands and sucked our clits until we came again.

I came to myself hearing a gentle knocking on the door. I was so sore and sated, exhausted tears of joy streamed down my face. I glanced at the nightstand. The candle was almost gone.

"I love you," I whispered, shuddering as she said the same words to me.

"Can I stay?" this time the words were only mine.

"You could," she said quietly. "But if you do, you'll be trapped here, an unknown woman with no wealth and no protection, in a time I fear is much more brutal to our kind than yours is. There's no guarantee you'd be able to be with me, and, more importantly, to return to my rooms next year during the gathering—unless you come to me again through the mirror." She kissed my clit, sucking it as she pulled her fingers free. I mirrored her movement, my flesh so tender, the pain so delicious, I felt her tears on my thigh, and mine falling on hers.

"Will you come back to me?" She said the words as I said, "I'll come back to you."

We smiled through our tears, quickly dragging our chemises back over our heads, letting the soft, worn linen fall quietly down around us. Holding hands, we walked to the table by the mirror. My reflection drew back the curtains. My sister and great-aunt were still in the room, both of them with their hands on their hips. The rattling on the door was growing louder. A woman's voice called insistently. The door was starting to open. The candle guttered.

"We're not like the others." My reflection whispered in my ear as she helped me onto the table. "Any time you love yourself in the mirror, I'll feel everything you do, even when I can't touch myself. You'll feel the same, too, when I love myself."

I glanced at the women waiting for me beyond the mirror. The door creaked open in back of us. A woman's voice was calling out.

"I love you," she said, kissing me hard and fierce, pushing me into the glass.

"I love you," I said, and walked through the veil of water that was the mirror. My feet touched silk, and I started to cry.

I turned and blew my reflection a kiss, smiling through my tears as I touched my cheek to take her kiss back to me. My sister and my aunt walked up beside me and slipped their arms around my shoulders, as the women in the mirror did to my reflection. The glass shimmered, and the air in the room was suddenly different, like the whole castle had gone quiet. May Day was over.

"Mirror portals don't open for many people," my aunt said, giving my shoulder a comforting squeeze. "My second cousin's grandmother was the last one, if I remember correctly. She gave us a bit of a fright a time or two, too, especially when she was in her eighties, waiting until the last possible moment to come back."

She kissed my cheek, sat me down on the chair, and motioned my sister to hand me a glass of brandy.

"Drink it up, dear. Apparently, you're starting early with the last minute business. Just be careful not to cut things too closely. If your reflection's guardian back then is anything like most of his cohorts, there's no telling what kind of an asshole he'd try to marry you off to back there. Our world isn't perfect, but it's a helluva lot better than the good old days."

I nodded, not even trying to hide the tears still streaming hot and silent down my face.

"Come to bed, dear. It's late, and if I remember correctly, a good stiff drink and a full night's sleep are what you need, now."

They settled me onto the pillows and under the covers. My sister set my book beside me, then dimmed the bedside lamp to a quiet glow. They walked quietly out of the room, closing the door behind them.

Almost by rote, I flipped through the pages, pausing in spite of myself to smile at the familiar faces still smiling back at me in the dim light of the room. As my eyes adjusted to the light, I could just barely make out the bed and my nightgown, and finally my face in the shadows of the glass. The light glowed warmly, reflecting back into the room. I touched my fingertips to my nipple, gasping as sensation screamed through the tip—and my fingers?

Oh, yes! I could feel her still. My reflection was masturbating along with me. I kicked off my covers, tore open my bodice, and pulled up my nightgown. My pussy was wet and hungry. In the mirror, my reflection's was, too. I could see her circling her clit as I circled mine. I sank back, laughing, into the pillows, and proceeded to love us both through the mirror.

Into Tipera
Kathleen Tudor

"You're not fucking listening to me!" Beverly screeched.

I sighed and clenched my jaw. "Have you seen my shoes?" I fully admit that it was a stupid thing to say. Beverly grabbed them from the floor by her feet and threw them at me overhand, and I ducked to let them hit the bulkhead before I bent, scooped them up, and laced them on. "Look, I'm sorry that you're having trouble getting funding for the hydro research. I'm not exactly having the easiest time myself, right now."

"That's my point," she hissed. "Your troubles are killing my side projects. No one wants to take a risk on the research assistant to a—" She let herself break off. She didn't really have to say it, anyway.

"A failure? A laughingstock? My principles are sound, Bev. We just need to figure out how to test it."

"You're going to have to figure it out for yourself," she finally said, deflating. I felt my heart patter twice, fast, and then sink. Had it stopped beating altogether? It might as well have.

"You can't mean that," I tried, though I knew better.

"I'm sorry, Redele, it's over. We're over. I've already started to look for another research posting. I'll leave as soon as I can confirm a position." She shrugged apologetically, but I refused to be softened.

"Nice. Guess I should have known better than to trust you." Not that she'd ever done anything to be less than worthy of my trust. Not that she'd even truly betrayed me. We were lovers, but there was no commitment—no contract. She was perfectly within her rights to run from my sinking ship while she still could. But that didn't make it hurt any less. I turned and stormed from the room that we would no longer share.

The station where we worked was small and sparsely populated, so I didn't pass many people as I rushed down the corridors to my lab. I ducked my head whenever I heard footsteps, knowing that my flushed face would only make my ruddy cheeks look splotchy and unhealthy. My hair fell forward around my face, further hiding me, and I managed not to be noticed at all on my way to the heavy bulkhead doors that marked the boundary to my own, private research lab.

My console woke as the computer detected me in the room, showing me the formulae I'd been working on for years now. I knew them all by heart by now, but I was no closer to proving them, despite the probe we'd just wasted a couple of months before. They should work. The drive I'd constructed should open up some kind of portal. But to where, it was impossible to say, and the damn thing required so much energy to work that we had to fly the probe—or ship—into a star to power it. Even with modern shielding tech, that was a tall order, and if the portal didn't open, there wasn't much chance of escaping the gravity well.

I was sure that the probe had made it, but telemetry had stopped as soon as the portal drive had activated. Wherever it had gone, it was too far away for us to reach by traditional means. What we needed was a pilot who could travel through the portal, return, and report back. But without a successful unmanned test, we couldn't get approval to hire a pilot, and without a pilot, we were never going to get a successful test. My career and my reputation had been staked on getting around that problem, and there was no solution in sight.

I moved to a second display, which showed live feed of the sleek little shuttle I'd prepared for the first manned flight. It would probably be dismantled and the parts redistributed to other research projects on the station, soon. My funding was running out, and my backers were not pleased with my lack of progress.

"I'm ruined," I said, tracing my fingers over the screen, tasting the words. Yes, ruined. And alone.

I shut the screen off, but the image of the shuttle was burned into my eyes, whispering to me of glory and accolades in the scientific community. I would be written of in the most

prestigious journals, not with derision as a failure, but as a vision-
ary. A genius! If only I found some way to get a pilot into that
damned shuttle.

"No," I whispered, but the idea had taken firm root. No, I
couldn't. But why not? I glanced around the cool lab, arms crossed
over my body for warmth and comfort. What would be left for
me if my residence in this little corner of the galaxy was taken
away?

I made the decision, and from there I didn't allow myself a
second thought. What else was there to think about, anyway?
With Bev giving up on me, my last human tie had been severed,
and I was sick of trying to make new ones. Instead, I would make
history.

I thought, for a moment, about whether to send a message
letting the station authorities know where I had gone, but
dismissed it. I would either come back to tell them myself, or I
would be dead and gone, and what would it matter after that,
anyway? No, better to go boldly. Now.

I hurried into the connecting passage to the private airlock
where the shuttle was stored, and climbed aboard. There were no
provisions. That was worrisome, at first—what if I came out in
between stars in some distant place?—but it would take too long
and call too much attention to me if I stopped to stock it. I
shrugged it off, praying that nothing so small would stop me, and
strapped myself into the pilot's seat with a feeling of finality.

In all correctness I should have filed some sort of flight plan or
request for departure, but our station saw almost no space traffic
except for our regular supply shuttles, and there wasn't one
scheduled for days. I took a deep breath and hit the release for the
airlock, and watched as the great bay door opened and the stars
whirled slowly by outside. I held my breath for a moment—
instinctively reacting to the view—and then let it out with a slow
sigh.

"Goodbye," I whispered. Then I charted a course for Tipera, our
own pretty, little sun, and engaged.

I had hours to regret my impulsive decision as I hurdled toward the star, but I would feel all the more foolish and hopeless if I turned around to go back, so I stuffed down the feelings of foolishness and fear and tried to keep hope foremost in my mind. This would work. It must. It would.

I triple-checked the shielding as the star grew to fill the light-filtered viewscreen ahead of me. It was like flying into hell, the surface flaming and boiling. My entire body shook with horror as I plunged into the inferno. I was dead. Oh, God, what a foolish, prideful thing, to fly into the heart of a sun! Death was the best I could hope for!

But as the blue-white glow filled the cabin, despite the dimmed screen, I took hold of my senses with both hands, prayed for a chance, even a tiny one, and then turned off the screen. With that sight of beautiful horror gone, I could focus on the control panel and the things I needed to do if I had any hope of surviving.

The portal drive charged, and I took a deep breath, waiting. Was it my imagination, or had it grown stifling in the cabin of the small ship? I imagined that I could feel myself begin to blister and burn in the heat. And then I hit the control to send my ship through the portal, and realized I'd been so very wrong.

My entire body burned with searing, agonizing heat. I flung myself from my seat and onto the shuttle floor, my voice a harsh scream, my eyes blind to my surroundings as I thrashed and burned. I could feel the fire licking at every inch of my skin, but why, oh why was it taking so long to die?

Then the heat started to fade, and I lay panting on the floor of the shuttle, still writhing in the memory of pain, my skin unmarked and clean. I stared at my arm in shock, wondering how it could be that I was in one piece, my skin white and smooth.

White? Smooth?

I looked again, my other hand rising to brush against the unblemished flesh. Where my skin had been rough and freckled before, now it was soft and clear. I shuddered, shaking off the last of the pain, but I couldn't seem to tear my eyes away from my arm. And were my fingers just a little longer and narrower? Surely the nails were glossier and better cared-for than I had ever managed to keep them.

My radio crackled, and I jerked, making my glossy auburn hair cascade around my face. Since when had it been so shiningly pretty? The reddish undertones that had shown up only in bright sunlight before were more evident, now, and the whole mess was smoother and healthier than I had ever seen it. The radio crackled again, demanding a response, and I climbed forward and tapped in the command to answer.

"Redele."

"Thank God! Are you okay? How did it go?" Bev's voice was tight with worry and breathless with anticipation, and I had to take another moment to steady myself against the surprise before I answered. If she knew I'd left, why hadn't she tried to stop me before I went into the star? Maybe I had been unconscious after the pain...

"Well, I survived," I said. "I'm heading back."

"I'll be waiting," she said. The promise in her voice made me sigh with longing, and I pinched myself for it. That ship had sailed.

I signed off and scrubbed my hands through my hair. My soft, lightly scented hair. What the hell?

But the mirror in the lav showed me that the hair and the arms were the least of it. Oh, I still looked like myself. But I looked like a better version of myself. Brighter, more symmetrical, maybe, and neatly groomed where I had allowed myself to grow ragged or shaggy before. My hair was neatly trimmed instead of growing uneven and splitting. My eyes seemed brighter, the color more vivid and the whites shining. My lashes were longer, my cheekbones just a fraction higher and more defined, and my waistline perhaps a bit trimmer.

It took nearly the entire return journey to come to terms with the slightly more perfect me in the mirror, each tiny change almost inconsequential on its own, but the many changes added up to a radically more beautiful woman in my reflection.

I jumped when the cockpit controls alerted me to the fact that

I was approaching the station. My fingers shook on the controls as I steered my way back into my small bay. Inside, Bev grinned and waved to me from behind a viewing panel, and I waved slowly back, wondering what she would make of my changed appearance. But as the air rushed back into the lock and the ship's hatch opened, she didn't seem to notice. Instead, she rushed through at the first opportunity, and threw herself into my arms.

When I jumped, shocked, she stepped back and smiled sheepishly at me. "I'm sorry," she said, "I know you don't like PDA, but I'm just so glad you're okay. Did it work? I registered the charge, but then it just sort of fizzled, and you shot out of the corona. I was so scared I was going to lose you when the ship didn't vanish!" She pressed a kiss to my cheek before stepping back.

"Um, it's okay," I told her. "It was terrifying. I guess I must have hit the engines at the last second."

"Thank goodness you're a quick thinker." I nodded, confused, and started to walk toward my lap, but the station seemed to tip under my feet, and I fell. Bev caught me and steadied me. "Oh, gosh! It's okay. Help me get her to her room; she should be lying down after all that!"

I finally noticed that a familiar face was hovering behind Bev, concerned. Mith. He'd been my junior research assistant, before dwindling funds and unhappy patrons had forced me to let him go. What was he doing here?

Whatever he was doing, it involved listening to Bev. He hurried forward and stooped to get one of my arms around his neck, and the two of them half-carried me back to my apartment. I stiffened in shock yet again when I saw it. Instead of a dull, dreary room, there were homey touches everywhere. A tapestry had been hung on one wall. A flickering glow-light candle rested on the small table by the couch where Mith and Bev laid me. The room smelled very faintly of... berries?

"You can go; I'll take care of her," Bev said. "Just take the rest of the day off, and we'll go over the data tomorrow."

He left silently, and I closed my eyes, still feeling dizzy. My skin flushed hot and then seemed to freeze, and I wondered if I was flushed or shivering.

"You've been through so much," Bev said quietly. She brought me a glass of juice, no doubt infused with her personal energy cocktail, and I sipped it gratefully, breathing in deep and savoring the taste of mango and orange.

"I'm okay, really. Just tired and a little dizzy. This will fix me right up." I waited to see if Bev would leave, but I was beginning to suspect that there was more to the differences in my life than just an improvement in my appearance. That was confirmed when Bev sat down next to me, squeezed onto the edge of the couch, and gently pet my hair as I finished the juice.

Her hair smelled like flowers and something softly exhilarating, like sea air. "You smell good," I said, half because it was true, and half because I wanted to see how she would react.

I heard the smile in her voice as she leaned into me. "You must have scrambled your brain in that star," she teased. So... still lovers, then?

I opened my eyes enough to peek through my lashes. "I don't think so," I said. I was already feeling better—stronger. "But I'm worried about what it means for the project."

"It'll be fine; stop worrying. Anyway, no one will touch your pet project. AmaCorp isn't going to do anything to upset you since you created that energy cell and gave them your exclusive license. They'd probably do just about anything to make sure you renew it in three years."

I remembered that project. I'd started it years ago, but dismissed it as less interesting and groundbreaking than my portal engine. Anyone could build a better power cell, but who was working on the kind of pure mathematical brilliance that was my engine? I might have kicked myself for dismissing the power cell project out of hand, but apparently, in this world, I'd put the need to make a living slightly ahead of the need to make a name for myself. Good for me.

"You always know how to make me feel better," I said.

Apparently it was true, because Bev gave a pleased little smile and leaned over me to press her soft lips to mine. Finally, here was something familiar! Her lips tasted sweet and felt soft and full against my own as she kissed me, sweetly at first, and then with more hunger. After a moment, she took a deep breath through her nose, and I felt the way she softened against me—a classic sign of her arousal. Some things were delightfully the same, it seemed.

I pulled back just enough to speak. "Do you want to get a little more comfortable?" And that was all it took. Bev helped me up, laughing as she pulled me to my feet. Her eyes traveled over me for a moment, assessing, but when I proved that I could stand unassisted, she reached for me and pulled me toward the bedroom.

"Better believe I do," she murmured into my ear. Then she nipped at my earlobe, and I felt the familiar shudders of pleasure go through my body at the contact. Sweet, familiar, erotic sensation coursed through my nerves, and I purred approval as we reached the bed. I nearly tripped onto it, and Bev clung to me, steadying and caressing all at once.

I laughed as I caught my balance, and then started to pull her clothes away. She grabbed at mine, and our hungry hands made quick work of the cloth. She caressed my breasts as they were freed to the cool air in the bedroom, and I felt my nipples rise to peaks beneath her seeking fingers. I pulled her closer and let my own fingers drift lower, brushing through her tight curls until I found the sweet nectar that they concealed.

Her taste exploded over my tongue as I brought my fingers back to my lips, and she gave a soft hum of pleasure when I trailed them back down her side and into her heat and wetness. "You're delicious," I said. She laughed and pulled me close for a kiss, her tongue sweeping over mine as if to take back the taste of her.

We stood that way for a long time, or tongues playing over one another, our hands roaming, our bodies growing heated despite the coolness of the room. I held back my hunger as long as

I could, savoring this new/old experience, and when I couldn't wait any longer, I teased my fingertips over the hard bud of her clit. Bev trembled, and I pressed again, harder, seeking the rhythm that made her sing against me.

My knuckles brushed against my own flesh, and I got yet another jolt of surprise when I found the flesh there bare to my touch. I'd apparently undergone hair removal treatment... I pressed my hips forward, letting the back of my hand stroke my own smooth flesh as I brought Bev closer and closer to the peak of her pleasure. It was a delight to explore my own body along with hers and to discover a new and enticing sensation in my own body even as I drove my lover toward her familiar moment of release.

"Come for me, baby," I whispered. She loved to hear me talk to her while we were getting it on, but I was usually too shy. Perhaps I could make a few conscious changes to go along with the new me. "Come, on, come for me. I want your sweet cream all over my fingers."

She gasped and arched even more sharply into my hand, pressing her whole body against me as she threw her head back and let out a long, low moan of satisfaction. Her body trembled in my arms, and I tightened my grip to keep her on her feet, though I didn't let up on that tiny spot of pleasure. Her cream did indeed flood over my fingers as I eased away from her clit and dipped between her folds. I slid one finger inside her, just to feel her clench around me, and sighed in pleasure.

When she was finished with her sighing and trembling dance, Bev lowered her head to my neck and kissed and nipped with a passion. "I'm so hungry for you," she said. And with a little shove, she'd knocked me back onto the bed. I scooted away, making room for her, and was surprised when she crawled between my legs instead of moving up beside me on the bed.

Ah, yet another thing that I had been too shy to indulge in most of the time. I felt so silly being the center of attention, lying on my back doing nothing while she—oh my God—with her tongue. I squirmed under the new assault, determined to enjoy myself and my shiny new self. It wasn't hard when she was apparently so talented. Had I really been too wrapped up in myself to notice, before?

I cried out as she slid two fingers inside me, curling them into the perfect shape inside me and stroking as she teased at my clit. She laughed as I bucked against her, apparently surprising her with my sensitive reaction, and the vibrations of her laughter nearly sent me into orbit. The way her face felt as she brushed against my bare skin was shocking and exciting, and I closed my eyes and let the sensations wash over me, bathing me in pleasure. And for the first time with this kind of pleasure, I relaxed enough to feel the wave of orgasm begin to coil inside of me like a dragon waking.

I shuddered and twitched beneath her, my cries growing louder as I absorbed each new sensation until the dragon burst free and my body trembled with my release. It was beyond anything I had ever experienced before. Is this what I had been missing for so long? The shyness reasserted itself in those moments, though, and I decided that the new me could take a tiny break from exercise of confidence. I pulled Bev up beside me and she came eagerly, tangling herself into my arms and locking her lips on mine so that I could taste my own sweet tang on her tongue.

We lost hours that night, locked together in pleasure as I shocked her with my hunger, and she returned it point for point. We both drifted off in the early hours of the morning, but I woke less than an hour later, my heart pounding, and I knew what I had to do.

I crept from my bed and accessed the files on my project. A few alterations to key parts of the formula would ensure that no one would ever be able to replicate my portal—at least not with my data. It was harder to alter the records in the shuttle, but I was its designer, after all, and I made sure that anyone looking at the flight data would see that I flew into the sun, charged the drive, and then had to divert the energy to my standard drives when the portal failed to open.

I climbed back into bed and wrapped my arms around my lover, already dreaming of another project and a new avenue of exploration. As for the portal... there was no going back.

Game Fae
Vivien Jackson

"I hear they let you go home after ten hours if you have kids, or even a pet to feed."

"Cinches it. Totally going to the pet store during my smoke break. You want me to pick up a hamster for you, dude?"

"Fuck no. You heard one of them things screech? Sound like my ex. What's the going rate on a bird?"

"Talking or not talking?"

Kyra listened to her two officemates chat, and her back curled lower and lower over her desk. Her index finger vibrated atop her ergo mouse. She tried not to think of how much she needed to ice down her wrists. Sleep kept pulling her eyelids downward, but she fought that bastard back. No way was she gonna let something as pussy as a need for sleep get in her way. This was her chance, her big opportunity: technical artist, not even contract, on a triple-A game title for a major studio. Her name up near the top of the credits. She had to nail this.

On the screen, she wrapped a new texture over the wire-frame model of this level's Big Bad. Pretty. Too pretty? Not edgy enough?

In her periphery, Zach knuckled his eyeballs. He hadn't shaved in weeks and looked yeti-like. She heard David yawn. Or groan, or something else she knew she didn't want to see. The guys were probably just as tired as she was, crunching for, what, seven weeks now? Fourteen-hour days, no weekends, bennie-prizes for people who stayed even later, longer, who put the pedal to the metal, put the 'we' in 'team,' and embodied other lame-sounding corporate speak, all with the goal of getting this game out the door.

Kyra tried to have sympathy for Zach and David and all the other guys working on Bad Fairy, but really, they were guys. They couldn't possibly get it. None of them had ever been the only chick in the uni computer science department. The only. None of them had ever deliberately cooled blushes when they rolled in one morning at god o'clock only to find that somebody had left a furry-muff porn screen saver up. On three monitors.

Nobody else in this whole damn building had to pretend that wasn't a turn-on. The guys, they just laughed it off, ribbed each other. Great fun, yeah.

Kyra's eyes glazed over, and she realized that her cursor had stopped moving. Weird. Her cursor never stopped moving, drawing, creating. It was a digital extension of her finger, of her imagination. It always did what she commanded. How could it be still? From a detached place at the very end of her string, she realized she was falling asleep. Sitting up. In her office chair. Zach and Dave were still talking, but they were no longer making words.

And then the office door leaned open, letting in a blade of fluorescent light from the hallway... and Lily.

Kyra woke up. Every fucking cell in Kyra woke up.

Lily was the Kevin-the-producer's assistant. She topped out at about five feet, had soft-looking, curly black hair and a killer little bod. But the really electric thing about her was her smile. She was always doin' it, too, grinning, even before the first pot of coffee, even after the last cleaning-crew vacuum sweep. Lily was always here, bubbly, keeping everybody's spirits up. Fetching things for Kevin, and for everybody, really. Kyra'd wondered more than once if she slept here.

Except that line of thought could get her in trouble because she'd start thinking about Lily in pajamas, then smaller pajamas, then slinky small pajamas... and her thoughts went down the gutter from there.

"How's it going?" Lily trilled, hauling all that light in from the hallway, but warming it up like natural sunshine. It crackled off Kyra's monitors, bleaching and flattening her game model. "Big Bubba's tonight, y'all. Tell me you don't yearn for BBQ."

"Just potato salad for me. Biggest vat of the stuff, please."

"Chopped beef, no pickles no onions no sauce no bread."

Leave it to Dave and Zach, respectively, to be totally unaffected by Lily's innuendo. Or maybe her words weren't really innuendo-laden. Maybe that was just Kyra's sleep-deprived brain supplying the breathy tone, the secret flirt. She liked how Lily had used the initials, not sounding out "barbie-que" and instead leaving some uncertainty there. BBQ... bright beveled quark? Big boobie queen? Bodacious buxom... oh, quit.

Lily leaned back against Kyra's desk and slid a menu onto it. Kyra tried not to notice the shallow impression the Formica edge pressed into Lily's skirt-covered ass.

"What can I get you, Ky?" See? There it was again, the breathy. The sexy. Only now Kyra could smell her, too. Not perfume, not even scented deodorant. Lily smelled like... lilies. Like walking in a garden right after the rain. That smell clanged so hard against the reality of Kyra's cave-like office that she almost got choked up. She wetted her lips and tried to scan the folded paper menu.

"Smoked turkey's good," Lily said. "That's what I'm having. And lots and lots of sauce."

Kyra felt her face get hot. Damn, she couldn't even summon the social acumen to order crappy crunch food. Was the job killing her, or had she always been this pathetic? She nodded and tried to say, "Yeah, sure, same for me," but it came out grunty.

She expected Lily, with her orders in hand, to rush off in her usual pixie scamper and start fetching things. Instead, Lily turned, faced the computer screen, and flattened her palms on Kyra's desk. LED light turned her face into a play of blues and deep pinks.

"She's hot, kind of in a domme way. I dig the leather flail." Lily was looking hard at the screen, but Kyra had clean forgotten what she was even working on. Or where she was. Lily's elbow brushed Kyra's shoulder, and sparks settled all over that side of her body.

"Yeah. Figured a fae wouldn't use a metal weapon, right?"

"Mmhmm. But..." Lily caught her bottom lip between her teeth for a second, and she turned to look straight at Kyra. Holy shit. Kyra couldn't even breathe. Her nipples peaked, and her toes scrunched up against the rubber of her flip-flops. "...you shouldn't make her wings red." Lily leaned in until her mouth was close, too close to Kyra's ear, and she whispered, "Fae wings only get red during orgasm. Blood flow and all that."

And then Lily was straightening up, retrieving the menus, reciting everybody's orders, and breezing back out into the hall. The door closed behind her, cocooning the game makers—two programmers, one tech artist—into their own dank little hell. Kyra almost convinced herself that she'd imagined that last part. Hallucinated it, really. After all, David and Zach were back to work like nothing even a little bit strange had happened.

But then she sucked in a breath, and the smell of flowers shoved her right back into that imaginary garden, and she knew that it had been real. Lily had literally, really, whispered into her ear.

Took Kyra about a minute to remember the contents of that whisper, and when she did, she decided she needed a smoke break. Right now. Didn't even matter that she didn't smoke.

Kyra was the only person on the fourth floor who used the ladies' bathroom. She knew this because once, just as an experiment, she'd held off telling anybody when the toilet paper ran out, and had just brought in little tissue packets for her own use. Three weeks went by before anybody thought to re-stock the ladies' room. She'd decided against performing a similar experiment that time when the overhead light went out. She wasn't hung up on her looks or anything, but every once in a while she needed to check her hair.

Lily must use the upstairs facilities. Made sense. Kevin's office was on five, right next to the super-secret executive board room. Lily probably had a desk up there, someplace.

At the sink, Kyra shoved her hands under a stream of cold water, got them good and wet, and then palmed her face. She felt hot, burning up, but buzzing like she'd just downed a half dozen Starbucks ventis. The faucet water didn't even begin to cool her down.

Her hands slid down, wrapping her throat, feeling the pulse push hard against her fingertips.

Thing was, even if she hadn't been deprived of sleep and real company—Zach and David didn't count—for almost two months, she still would have wanted to fuck Lily. This wasn't some cracked fantasy she'd thought up to dull the craziness of her work schedule. In fact, that first day last summer when Kevin had introduced her to his assistant, Kyra's mouth had flooded with wet, pooling up behind her teeth, and she'd wanted nothing more than to run her tongue all over Lily's body, to inhale and consume. It'd been all Kyra could manage to just half-smile and say hey.

And even then Lily's look had been knowing.

Could she? Could she really tell that Kyra lusted after her, and how hard? It wasn't the first thing on most women's minds when they met each other. Not that Kyra went around propositioning every succulent female who walked through her world—that would lead to heartbreak real fast—but she'd had enough romantic experience to be patient and make sure the other person was totally open to same-sex intimacy before she said anything remotely flirtatious. Most women, even those who'd been out a long time, approached relationships carefully. Kyra never wanted to offend.

But Lily had never let something like politeness hold her back. She'd been out of her bikini top before sundown at the company picnic. Granted, she was an equal-opportunity enticer, and could be bi, or even totally straight. After all, most guys were just as worked up about her as Kyra was. Only difference was that they could talk about it amongst themselves. They didn't feel a need to frig off in the bathroom, fantasizing about their co-worker. Or maybe they did. Kyra didn't really give a fuck.

Through drop-lidded eyes, she saw her reflection in the mirror. Her hair was coming out of its ponytail one strand at a time. It licked her forehead and neck, fringed her ears. Her face looked flushed, and she could see her nipples pushing hard through her bra and tee-shirt, just begging for someone to touch them. Kyra kept one hand around her throat, feeling the heat of her skin burn through her palm. The other hand crept south, over her tee-shirt, roving her bra, pinching one nipple, harder, and pulling it until she mewled.

She imagined Lily touching her like this.

She narrowed her eyes at her reflection, seeing herself as Lily would see her, and the background blurred. The dusky pink wall behind her closed in, embracing her, framing her. Fantasy gave that frame a shape: dark pink fairy wings, deepening to red.

Blood flow and all that, was it?

Kyra reached with both hands and grabbed her breasts, kneading, rolling her nipples until they burned. She needed more, needed other hands than hers, but this was all she had. She yanked her tee-shirt up and unbuttoned her jeans, flaying them over her sharp hip bones, exposing her trim, white panties. One hand dipped in. She saw the point of her knuckle and felt the fingernail graze her lips, her clit. She sucked in a breath and clutched the faux marble vanity with the other hand to keep herself upright.

Her middle finger slipped along the seam of wet, seeking the depths of her cunt, but the jeans still limited her access somewhat. Never mind, she could get off just rubbing her clit. And watching. And imagining that Lily was also watching. And touching. And coming, watching her. Kyra's hips tilted, driving into her fingers. She pressed her clit so hard that, were it another body part, she'd be leaving bruises for sure.

She climbed closer to release, so close, so hard that for a half-breath she didn't register the vibration against her thigh. And then, even when she realized that her phone was humming, her first thought was that, hey, that might feel good on her clit, shuddering her fairy wings to crimson. She just needed... Kyra let go of the vanity and pushed at the phone—still inside her jeans pocket—cramming it in toward her pussy, clamping her teeth as it grated over her hip bone. Fuckity-fuck: the pocket just wasn't wide enough. She yanked the phone out. Her fingers were already aiming it down her panties when she peeked at the illuminated screen.

A message from Kevin: *Kyra, 2 my office plz.*

Fuck.

❈

Kevin's door was open. It was always open. That was his policy. Sometimes the old farts tried too hard to be cool. Kyra rapped her knuckles on the door frame.

Some butterflies had set up shop in her belly, even though there was no way Kevin could know how she'd been spending her smoke break. If he knew, after all, that meant cameras in the bathroom, which was legally not cool. But Kevin wasn't the peeper type. Or was he? It hit Kyra all at once that maybe she wasn't the only person around here keeping secrets.

"Hey? You needed to see me?"

Kevin had his flip-flop-shod feet up on his desk and a tablet balanced on his thigh. When he looked up and saw Kyra in his doorway, he gestured for her to come in. "Have a seat, Ky. You already have dinner?"

"Um, no. Lily just now came around taking orders. I figure food's about half an hour off."

Kevin reached out with an unnaturally long arm and slid a dish along the desk. It was piled with cut fruit, and the waft hit Kyra's nose full force. Her mouth watered, and suddenly she was horribly, starkly, gut-churningly hungry. She sat down opposite Kevin and grabbed a mango wedge from the dish.

But eating one bite just made her hungrier. She shoved a second into her mouth, swiped the back of her hand across her lips, and forced herself to keep from reaching for more food. Despite some disturbing noises coming from her belly, she really didn't need to gorge right here in her boss's office.

"Better?" Kevin closed the tablet case and set it on a side table. Kyra nodded.

"How's the level boss coming?"

Gotta change the wings. "Nearly done. I'll send you a composite before I leave tonight. I can put together some mock-ups for marketing tomorrow, if they need something."

Kevin's eyebrows may have twitched slightly, but hell, they were so thick Kyra couldn't be sure. "Lily told me you were having some palette issues."

Lily what? A surge of panic nearly had Kyra out of her chair before she settled herself. No, no, Lily probably said something about colors, but no way had she told Kevin exactly what she'd said. Kyra looked down at her hands, picked a loose thread on her tee-shirt hem. "Nothing I can't handle. I'm surprised she mentioned it."

Kevin took his sweet time replying, and Kyra didn't dare look up. Finally, he drawled, "She's interested in you getting this world right, Kyra. I am, too."

"Sorry," Kyra mumbled. How had this conversation become a treatise on her lack of vision? She was still on edge, jumped up from her bathroom break, and her defenses were down. Bitterness spiked. She had half a thought of telling Kevin off—of telling him that if he was so determined to stamp his own vision on this game, he could fucking well go down to her cramped, dark little office and knock himself out for fourteen hours a day, seven days a week. She didn't need his shit. She needed... to calm down. Damn, damn, where was her usual control?

She heard his chair squawk as he shifted. "Can I show you something?"

Kyra looked up before she could stop herself. Kevin was standing, holding out a hand. For some reason, she had this weird *Matrix* flash: red pill, blue pill, rabbit hole. Kevin looked weird, out of time and place, something magical.

And that's when my brain goes pop. "Sure."

Kyra followed her boss out of his very normal-looking office, down the hall to the next door, and then into a horribly normal-looking board room. Kind of cramped, though. Not what she'd expected from the super-secret executive meeting room, the holy of holies, where all the money guys got together to discuss the future of the studio's projects. Kevin didn't stop at the black-lacquer table. He went right to the overhead projector, reached below it, and fiddled with something there.

The projection screen hummed back into the wall, leaving a giant floor-to-ceiling gap. A secret passage on the fifth floor, downtown. Holy crap. Kyra blinked, but the doorway was still there.

"If you're very still, sometimes you can hear them from here, but the sound quality is loads better if you actually, you know, go inside."

He didn't need to push. Kyra could almost hear... music. Well, rhythm. She could feel it beneath the soles of her flip-flops. She could feel it in her bones. And there, pitched pretty high, a tinkle of laughter. Or a song? It was like ear-bleeding technojunk had mated with Disney to produce this gorgeous whorl of sound. Kyra wanted to hear it louder, wanted to dance inside it. Not even caring whether Kevin came in behind her, she stepped through the gap in the wall.

And everything she knew about the world and physics and reality exploded.

Fifth floor? Office building? Try Palladian whorehouse disco heaven. Blurs on the air that were kind of like clouds bore trays of fruit a lot like the one back on Kevin's desk. A fountain off to the right gurgled with blue stuff, and the closer Kyra got to it, the more it smelled like cotton candy. In every space, dancers writhed to the music, blurring bodies. She tried to concentrate on seeing just one dancer, but such focus proved impossible in this mosh.

A few of those bodies were clothed. Most mouths were full, of food or bubbles or blue liquor or someone else's body. Contortions of touch blew away everything a teen-aged Kyra had once learned from the Kama Sutra. Nothing, not even gravity, limited these people.

As her gaze panned the room, she came to the middle of the palace temple chamber, and her attention snagged on a dais. Vines of glowing blue stuff reached up from the misty floor, forming drapery around a platform that looked like it was made of pearl. Kyra blinked again, and the flashes of glitter on the air—things she'd assumed on first glance were bugs or confetti—resolved into tiny people with wings. Fairies. A least a dozen of them. Their wings were made of flickering light, all pulsing in rhythm with the music.

"This is the world we're trying to share with the mortals," said a voice from behind her left shoulder. Took Kyra a minute to connect that voice with Kevin. He sounded different here— different timbre. And then she realized that he didn't sound at all. Her ears were still full of the throbbing, piercing music, so full she couldn't possibly hear a plain, old human voice. Instead, Kevin seemed to be speaking directly into her mind. The sensation of voice was accompanied by a lick of heat along her spine. Sensory overload?

"Keep going. You're almost there."

Kyra did as instructed, rounding a pillar as she approached the pearl-topped dais and the edge of the vine canopy. And then she saw.

Slim foot, toenails varnished black. Round of calf, bent knee. And another leg, dangling over the far side of the platform. Kyra put her hand out and grasped the column for support, but she couldn't force her mouth shut as she looked her fill.

Lily, atop a mound of that blur-cloud stuff, her hair rioting over the pearl, her wrists bound by those slender blue vines. A fairy latched onto one breast, suckling it, whirring the air with the flutter of his—her? —wings. And as Kyra watched, another fairy flew in, attached itself to Lily's other nipple. Two more joined, nibbling, stroking with their tiny hands. For all the furious flutter, those wings also kept time with the music. Kyra wasn't even sure how it happened—she didn't know much about music, honestly—but hell, if gravity here was optional, maybe syncopation was, as well.

"She's fucking gorgeous," Kyra murmured.

"She's their queen."

The white of the pearl glimmered, mottled, and Kyra saw a flash of blue snake through it. On the dais, Lily opened her mouth and spread her legs wide open. Three fairies ducked into the lee between her thighs. Kyra tried for a better angle to see, but she could guess what they were doing. Her own clit thrummed in time. Clothes felt like bandages, bindings, shackles.

"It's okay. You can take them off."

Kyra forced herself to look away from the sumptuous display Lily was offering, but Kevin wasn't behind her anymore. She wasn't sure where he'd gone, but it didn't matter. She didn't feel abandoned. She didn't worry about getting back to the board room. Honestly, she didn't worry about anything. The music had invaded her blood, and the waft of cotton candy now carried an under-whiff of something dark and molten, patchouli and cannabis and... lilies. Well, of course, right? Dark lilies, though. Blossoming in sighs from the queen on the dais, rising as her chest rose with breath, unfurling from between her dew-damp thighs.

Kyra didn't remember taking her clothes off, but when she reached down to stroke her nipples, no tee-shirt got in the way. Thank God.

"Come up here. With me." The voice in her head wasn't Kevin anymore. It was Lily. "Come up here and show me what you're doing, Ky. Let me feast my eyes."

Kyra mounted the dais and found herself surrounded by fairies. They moved too fast for her to discern their sex, but things like gender identity seemed as bendable as physics here. No male/female, just bodies moving together, pleasuring and being pleasured in one mass of delight. Kyra had sworn off dick a long time back, but if one had slipped in from behind in that moment, she wouldn't have minded. Her whole body was electrified, ablaze and needing. In this place, she wasn't alone, the only girl, the only gay girl, the only anything. She was part of the greater whole. Part of the faerie queen.

A tiny fae tugged at her earlobe, shishing into her ear, tweaking a sweet spot of sensation just below, next to her head. Another found the pulse point in her neck and rubbed against it. Felt like the rough tongue of a cat, but warm and slick.

God, to feel something like that on her clit.

Laughter trilled in her mind. "Now you're getting it. We aren't bad fairies, we just like fucking. Open your eyes."

Kyra obeyed, and the fairies moved away, offering her a clear view of Lily's gorgeous pussy. Fat lips trembled with dew, and the hard bulb of her clit jutted through like a seedling, ripe and ready for tasting. "Suck it, Ky."

She didn't need prompting. Kyra climbed up onto the dais— what had seemed hard as pearl and gorgeously iridescent, gave under her hands, like skin. Warm, slick, pulsing with the thrum of the music and her own heartbeat, now, all one rhythm. Kyra spread her palms against it and breathed in the musky smell, mocha and lilies and cinnamon and cream. She nuzzled against the inside of Lily's knee, covering her face with the smell, with the heat. Her teeth raked across hot flesh, nipping, gnawing up inner thigh, roughing the tender, tender skin. The musk grew headier, thicker, hotter, as her face approached Lily's cunt, and the music's rhythm shortened, stabbed the air. Rocked her insides.

She felt fairies swarm her body, slipping against sensation points she didn't even know existed: the small of her back, the arches of her feet, her navel, her ears and breasts and hip bones and ass cheeks and calves and elbows and clit and pussy... God. She writhed against them but they were all over, everywhere, and there was no way to get leverage, to set the rhythm, to increase or decrease the pressure according to her will. She had no will.

Her mouth found succor and lapped, drinking in Lily's dew, suckling that delicious clit. Her chin dripped, slid along Lily's cleft. Beneath her palms, the dais pulsed. It warmed, hotter and hotter. She hollowed her cheeks, pulling hard on Lily's clit, digging her chin into the divot of her cunt, smearing her face, blurring their bodies like all the others in this room, in this world.

Orgasm erupted from at least a dozen epicenters, and Kyra's body and brain and universe shuddered hard, parting into a million pieces and reforming, glued by the strangeness of this place, the fury of emotion and sensation. Two things tethered her through it: the steady pulsing pearl skin beneath her hands and the tensed, shuddering body beneath her mouth.

"Come, my queen," Kyra thought, but her mouth was way too busy to make words. Still, she felt that Lily heard. Her hands melted into her wrists, bathed in fire. The heat was unbearable, but she heard Lily shouting, calling, singing, pounding out the rhythm of her delight.

Kyra tasted deeper, and Lily came.

"Lean back and look. See me."

Kyra opened her eyes. It physically hurt to pull her face away from Lily's still-throbbing cunt. She'd been caffeine-free a whole day before and hadn't jonesed for a taste like this. But Lily had asked, and Kyra wasn't about to say no. Not after this.

She rose up on her hands, looked down. The dais, which she'd first thought was white and then later decided was translucent with pangs of blue, now glowed deep crimson, a deeper red than she had ever seen, even on a light box. True red, blood red. Fuck red.

And this wasn't a weird skin-covering on a hard dais. It had shape. Wing shape. Beneath Lily lay her wings, burning vibrant red, filled with heat and orgasm.

Kyra stroked them reverently, helping her lover down from climax, settling into the slowing music, slushing sensory soup. She brushed a kiss against Lily's thigh. Lily laughed.

"Now then, art-girl, I think you can draw faerie."

"Damn right," said Kyra. "Just let me check that red again."

Contributors

Annabeth Leong has written romance and erotica of many flavors—dark, kinky, vanilla, straight, lesbian, bi, and menage. Her work has appeared in the Circlet anthologies *Whispers in Darkness, Like a Midsummer Night*, and *Like Hearts Enchanted*, and more than twenty other anthologies. She lives in Providence, Rhode Island, blogs at annabethleong.blogspot.com, and tweets @AnnabethLeong

R. Ann Sawyer lives and works in New England, where she and her partner enjoy exploring the many meanings of the words "roleplay." She has always been entranced by the myriad things one can do with string.

Kate Dominic is a former technical writer who now writes about more interesting ways to combine slots and tabs. She is the author of over 400 erotic short stories. Kate had many Irish ancestors, though she has no proof any of them were time travelers.

Kathleen Tudor is currently hiding out in the wilds of California with her spouse and their favorite monkey. She should be considered armed with a pen and extremely erotic, and should be approached with caution. Her wicked words have already broken down the doors to presses like Cleis, Mischief HaperCollins, Circlet, Xcite, and more, and she is said to be disguising herself as an acquisitions and developmental editor for Storm Moon Press, where her first novella, *Hearts of the Hunted*, is available now. If you see her (or want to say hi!) please contact polykathleen@gmail.com. Keep an eye on KathleenTudor.com for updates on her antics and possible snippets of sexy material. This is her second anthology with Circlet Press.

Vivien Jackson has been copy editing for a long time and has some real clear opinions on the Oxford comma, that/which, and dangling participles. Lately, however, she's been concentrating on other kinds of dangly bits, fictionally speaking. She lives in Texas, speaks with a twang, and rustles Chihuahuas. She has a husband. Sometimes rustles him, too. Feel free to peek at www.vivienjackson.com.

More titles you may enjoy from Circlet Press!

One Saved To The Sea by Catt Kingsgrave
$3.99   ISBN: 978-1-61390-056-7

Lambda Literary Award Nominee & Winner of the 2012 Rainbow Award for Lesbian Paranormal Fiction.

Drawing on myth and history, Catt Kingsgrave writes a tale of the clash of the modern age with magic, of loss and searching, a tale that will sweep you away to a past that never was, and into a sapphic love story just this side of impossible.

Like A Queen
edited by Cecilia Tan & Rachel Kincaid
$5.99   ISBN: 978-1-885865-83-0

Five lesbian fairytales that feature classic stories, instead of competing for princes or beauty, the women in these stories are made more powerful by their desire for each other. What are the erotic possibilities of the enchanted princesses and forbidding queens that we learned about as children?

Women On The Edge Of Space
edited by Danielle Bodnar & Cecilia Tan
$3.99   ISBN: 978-1-61390-019-2

Lesbian women explore the inner depths of their sexuality while traveling through the reaches of outer space. In these four stories, women explore the uncharted trails of human desire as they rocket through space and transcend time and place, satiating a hunger for intimacy in a strange new world.

www.ingramcontent.com/pod-product-compliance
Lightning Source LLC
Chambersburg PA
CBHW020642130626
46552CB00003B/1365